A PRICE TOO HIGH

A Delta Force Unleashed Thriller

Also by J. Robert Kennedy

James Acton Thrillers

The Protocol
Brass Monkey
Broken Dove
The Templar's Relic
Flags of Sin
The Arab Fall
The Circle of Eight
The Venice Code
Pompeii's Ghosts
Amazon Burning
The Riddle
Blood Relics
Sins of the Titanic
Saint Peter's Soldiers
The Thirteenth Legion
Raging Sun
Wages of Sin
Wrath of the Gods
The Templar's Revenge
The Nazi's Engineer
Atlantis Lost
The Cylon Curse
The Viking Deception
Keepers of the Lost Ark
The Tomb of Genghis Khan
The Manila Deception
The Fourth Bible
Embassy of the Empire
Armageddon
No Good Deed
The Last Soviet
Lake of Bones
Fatal Reunion
The Resurrection Tablet
The Antarctica Incident
The Ghosts of Paris
No More Secrets
The Curse of Imhotep

Dylan Kane Thrillers

Rogue Operator
Containment Failure
Cold Warriors
Death to America
Black Widow
The Agenda
Retribution
State Sanctioned
Extraordinary Rendition
Red Eagle
The Messenger
The Defector
The Mole
The Arsenal

Just Jack Thrillers

You Don't Know Jack

Templar Detective Thrillers

The Templar Detective
The Parisian Adulteress
The Sergeant's Secret
The Unholy Exorcist
The Code Breaker
The Black Scourge
The Lost Children
The Satanic Whisper

Kriminalinspektor Wolfgang Vogel Mysteries

The Colonel's Wife
Sins of the Child

Delta Force Unleashed Thrillers

Payback
Infidels
The Lazarus Moment
Kill Chain
Forgotten
The Cuban Incident
Rampage
Inside the Wire
Charlie Foxtrot
A Price Too High

Detective Shakespeare Mysteries

Depraved Difference
Tick Tock
The Redeemer

Zander Varga, Vampire Detective

The Turned

A PRICE TOO HIGH

A Delta Force Unleashed Thriller

J. ROBERT KENNEDY

ISBN: 9781998005512

First Edition

For those members of the thin blue line that have lost their lives in the war against drugs, and the millions of innocent lives lost or destroyed because of the unchecked power of the cartels.

A PRICE TOO HIGH

A Delta Force Unleashed Thriller

"We cannot continue doing the same thing and expect different results."

Otto Perez Molina

"The war on drugs has gone on for about forty-five, fifty years - and it's been a complete failure. If you had a business that was failing so badly, you would change course. And it's just incredible that governments continue along the same course."

Richard Branson

PREFACE

The war on drugs, now decades old, has been an abject failure according to most analysts, and it is hard to disagree. However, what is the solution?

Hundreds of thousands have died in Mexico, murdered by the cartels, the profits from the sale of narcotics simply too high to give up. This was true during the time of Al Capone and Prohibition, as it is now. Some advocate decriminalizing drug possession, others go further and demand complete legalization of all narcotics.

And still others demand an even harsher response.

Declare the drug cartels terrorist organizations, send our military to actively pursue them, and bring justice to the masses.

It is an interesting concept.

And one wonders how the well-armed and financed cartels, estimated to directly employ over 450,000 people in Mexico, would react.

Thousands died in the gang wars during Prohibition.

Imagine the price with modern weaponry.

Mexico City, Mexico

One week from now

Sergeant Leon "Atlas" James gripped the handhold on the roof of the up-armored SUV, his M4 still smoking from the scores of 5.56x45 millimeter rounds he had delivered toward the enemy. Things were almost quiet on the streets of Mexico City now, the past hour having been brutal, but as the foot soldiers of the cartels were left behind, a sense of calm set in, the idea that they might actually make it out of this gauntlet alive taking hold.

And it was a dangerous idea. It meant complacency if he weren't careful. And he was in command at the front of the motorcade, with two world leaders relying upon him to get them to safety. His country was in disarray, reeling from an incomprehensible massacre. Thousands of innocents were dead across America, millions mourned, and if today were any indication, this new war his country found itself embroiled in would cost the lives of countless more, leaving an entire nation to grieve for what had been lost.

“RPG!” shouted one of the Canadian JTF 2 operators riding on the running board behind him.

Atlas turned slightly to his right and cursed as rocket fuel propelled the explosive warhead toward them. He glanced over to the other side of the vehicle at Niner, the best friend he had ever had, and said a silent apology for having led them directly into a trap as another RPG streaked toward them.

They had been waiting for them all along.

Belme Residence, West Luzon Drive

Fort Liberty, formerly Fort Bragg

North Carolina

Present Day

"I can't say I'm looking forward to the test, but I am looking forward to getting the results."

Maggie Dawson reached out and squeezed Shirley Belme's hand. "I'm sure everything will turn out fine. Even if it is cancer, you've caught it early."

Vanessa Moore put her cooler on a Moosehead Beer coaster. "How did you find the lump in the first place?"

Shirley grinned. "*I* didn't find it."

"Oh?"

"Red did."

Maggie snickered. "That's how I know I have nothing to worry about. BD gives the girls a good working over on a regular basis."

Vanessa laughed. "I hope you return the favor."

Maggie's eyes narrowed, puzzled, and Vanessa grabbed her crotch as if adjusting a hefty set. All three erupted in laughter, eliciting a response from the men clustered around the barbecue.

Sergeant Carl "Niner" Sung sauntered over. "Okay, who's cracking jokes? Everyone knows that's my job."

Maggie eyed Bravo Team's resident comedian. "We were talking about testicular cancer."

Atlas' eyes shot wide. "You laugh about something like that? That's kind of cold. It's like every man's nightmare."

Vanessa reached over and patted his boys. "Don't worry, dear. I checked you out thoroughly last night. You're okay."

He grinned. "So that's what that was all about."

Angela Henwood, Niner's girlfriend, walked up and waved. "Hey, everybody. Sorry I'm late. My replacement at the Exchange didn't show up. Apparently, she felt giving birth was more important than relieving me."

"The nerve!" cried Vanessa.

Niner agreed. "I thought these things were scheduled nine months in advance."

Maggie gave him a look then her head lolled toward Angela as she kissed her boyfriend. "You've got a lot to teach this boy."

"Evidently." Angela patted Niner's cheek. "I'll explain the birds and the bees to you later."

Niner smirked. "I hope it's a visual presentation with audience participation."

"Absolutely."

Niner flashed a toothy smile at Atlas. "I hope she checks for cancer."

Angela eyed him. "What the hell are you talking about?"

Niner waved a hand at the women. "I don't know. Ask them what they were laughing about."

Angela's hand darted to her chest. "Oh, Shirley, have you had your test yet?"

Shirley shook her head. "No, the mammogram is scheduled for tomorrow."

Angela shuddered. "Ugh. I had one of those once. So uncomfortable."

Niner regarded her. "Really? Isn't it just like an ultrasound or something of your tatas?"

Angela gave him the stink eye. "Classy. How about I put your sausage and meatballs in a panini press and see what you think."

Niner cooed. "Sounds fun!"

Atlas' eyes rolled. "You're forgetting, I shower with him. He wouldn't feel a thing."

Niner struck a pose, a single finger daintily placed on his chin as his eyes roamed Atlas' chiseled body. "So, you were looking?"

Atlas groaned. "I can't win." He threw up his hands and turned away, returning to the barbecue. "I just can't win with that guy."

Niner fired his finger guns after the big man then holstered them. "Like I said, making jokes is my job." He held up a finger, cocking an ear.

"What?" asked Maggie.

He pointed at the radio sitting nearby. "The president's giving a speech." He stepped over and turned the volume up as other members of Bravo Team, all part of what the public commonly thought of as the Delta Force, officially 1st Special Forces Operational Detachment—Delta, stopped what they were doing and clustered around the radio.

"*—and due to this ongoing crisis and the Mexican authorities' inability to deal with the situation, I have been forced to take action. Effective immediately, all Mexican drug cartels have been reclassified as terrorist groups. This reclassification opens up new avenues—*"

Niner's phone beeped, as did half a dozen others, and Maggie's chest tightened. He held it up. "Recalled."

Maggie rose. "What do you think it is?"

"Can't say for sure"—he gestured toward the radio—"but you just heard what the commander-in-chief said. Looks like we're going to war with the cartels."

1st Special Forces Operational Detachment—Delta HQ

Fort Liberty, North Carolina

A.k.a. "The Unit"

Command Sergeant Major Burt "Big Dog" Dawson stared at the latest satellite imagery displayed on a smart table. His commanding officer, Colonel Thomas Clancy, stood on the other side.

"What do you think? Can you do it?"

Dawson nodded. He had been planning the mission for a week. While America was just finding out what was about to happen, he had been in the know for some time. America had finally had enough and was reclassifying drug cartels as terrorists. It made sense. The cartels did far more damage daily to America than any terror group had, with the only exception 9/11, and the country had tried everything else and failed. Aside from giving up, escalation was the only other option. He just questioned whether it would be effective. "We can do it. It's risky, especially now that they know we're coming."

Clancy frowned. "Unfortunately, the president had no choice. The Mexicans are pissed about this."

"I wouldn't have bothered consulting them."

Clancy chuckled. "Which is why you're a soldier and not a diplomat."

"True. If a soldier were in charge, the risks would be a lot lower."

"If a soldier were in charge, we'd be living in a dictatorship."

Dawson raised a hand. "I meant a vet."

"I know what you meant, Sergeant Major, and you might be right. But in this case, we need to think of the long-term implications. My last briefing indicates the Mexicans are going to publicly endorse our actions, and thank us for our assistance. The Mexican president is scheduled to give a speech immediately after ours."

"Well, let's hope neither one announces when and where we're going in."

"I think we're safe there. And we're going to let them stew for a couple of days, wondering what's going on." Clancy sighed, folding his arms. "Unfortunately, even if we were going in without the president's announcement, they would have known we were coming anyway."

Dawson agreed. "The cartels have eyes everywhere." He indicated the satellite image of their target's compound. "We don't think he's going to go to ground?"

"Not this one. He's the most vocal and brazen of them all. Local police won't go near the area, and the military doesn't even do any flyovers. This group is extremely violent. I highly recommend if things go south, you don't allow yourself to be taken prisoner."

Dawson said nothing, his thoughts of Maggie. They were newlyweds with their entire lives ahead of them, and a mission like this with an enemy more vicious than the jihadists could swiftly put an end to all those plans.

Clancy leaned forward, lowering his voice. "I'm serious about this, BD. They will skin you alive."

Dawson was well aware of the risks. The cartels were notorious for being barbarians. "I'll keep it in mind, but if we have proper air cover, we should be able to get out of any situation we find ourselves in."

"You'll have air cover as discussed, but the intel indicates they might have Stingers. The key is going to be getting in and out as fast as you can, and staying undetected for as long as you can. Once they're able to mobilize a response, this thing gets a whole lot more difficult. If at any point you believe the mission can't be accomplished, you abort. I don't want good men dying when a sniper's bullet could do the job."

"It would make things a lot easier. Why aren't we just killing these people?"

"Because the president is pushing this as part of his law-and-order agenda. He wants trials. He wants these people who are worshiped by the men and women that work for them, and admired by too much of the Mexican population, to be humiliated."

"I have a feeling that if this operation goes bad, we'll be sending in hit squads to get the job done."

"It's highly unlikely we'll get out of this unscathed, and the American public will quickly grow tired of our brave men and women dying doing the job the Mexicans should be doing, and we both know that there's always someone to fill any vacant position."

Dawson grunted. "Kill enough lieutenants and then eventually there's no one to captain the ship."

"That's a lot of lieutenants."

Dawson shrugged and flashed a grin. "Better than sergeants."

Clancy laughed. "You're mixing your branches there, Sergeant Major." He frowned. "Just like we've been fighting the war on terror for decades now, I have a feeling we're about to get ourselves into something far worse."

Dawson stared at the map displayed on the wall indicating all the various targets for the upcoming mission. "Sir, I think we're about to start a war my grandchildren will be fighting."

Dawson Residence, Lake in the Pines Apartments

Fayetteville, North Carolina

"When will you be back?"

Dawson shrugged at Maggie's question. "I can't say. Shouldn't be too long."

His wife frowned. As Clancy's personal assistant, she was privy to far more than the other spouses. It gave him the freedom to be a little more open with what he said around her, but it also meant she didn't have the luxury of ignorant bliss. "I have a bad feeling about this one."

Dawson regarded her as he put down his fork, his plateful of lasagna forgotten. He had never heard her say anything like that before. She was obviously terrified. "What makes you say that?"

"These people are brutal. I've seen the news reports. They've killed tens of thousands, if not hundreds of thousands of innocent people that got in their way. I think this mission is a mistake. The reprisals could be unthinkable. You know how open that border is. They could send thousands of their people across and wreak havoc on our streets."

Dawson resumed eating. "For a minute there, I thought you were concerned something might happen to me."

She gave him a look. "This isn't my first rodeo. No good wife tells her husband before the big game that she thinks he's going to lose."

Dawson chuckled. "No, I suppose not. With respect to your fears, I agree. This isn't like going after the Taliban or Al-Qaeda or even ISIS. They're all on the other side of the world and have to go to some effort to get on our soil. But this is Mexico. This is our next-door neighbor. We've got a massive border where millions cross it every year illegally. We could be in for a world of hurt."

"Doesn't the White House realize that?"

Dawson took another bite, holding up his fork, signaling her to wait for his response. He swallowed. "I'm sure they do, and I'm sure they've weighed the risks. I know we've advised them it's a mistake. Not the mission, but the repercussions. Nobody goes into a fight like this thinking they're going to lose. Thousands are dying on the streets already due to the poison they peddle and the turf wars. This will make things worse, possibly far worse in the short term, but if we can turn the tide, we might be able to get the Mexicans more engaged so they take care of their own problem, and maybe we can put an end to some of this defund the police nonsense and hug-a-thug programs. This country needs to take crime more seriously. Enough with the wrist slaps."

"But aren't the prisons full?"

"You know what we did at Bragg when we were scaling up after 9/11 and ran out of barracks space?"

"What?"

"We built more barracks." He finished his plate and pushed it away, wiping his mouth with his napkin. "My God, that's the best damn lasagna I've ever tasted."

She smiled. "You say that every time."

"And I mean it every time."

"My mom's recipe."

"That woman is a saint."

"I'll tell her you said so."

"Do that."

"There's more if you want it."

He refused. "No, I don't want to be weighed down for the mission. Two helpings is already more than enough."

The oven timer beeped and Maggie rose, heading back into the kitchen.

"Oh, God, woman, what are you going to try to feed me now?"

She giggled. "It's not for you, it's for the boys. I made two extra trays for you to take to the Unit. Some of the guys rarely get a homecooked meal, especially the single ones, especially Spock…" Her voice cracked at the mention of the recent widower's name. Sergeant Will "Spock" Lightman had tragically lost his wife to Russian mobsters recently, and the Unit was still reeling from the loss. Though she wasn't a soldier, she was family.

Civilians on the outside didn't understand that the military was one big family, and those that served who had spouses and children that followed them around the world on their postings, who sat at home, glued to the television set, gripping the phone while praying the doorbell never rang with a chaplain on the doorstep, those husbands and wives, those children, they served their country as well. They kept the households running. They made sure things didn't fall apart at home while their loved one served in some foreign land to protect a way of life paid for with so much blood.

Dawson joined Maggie in the kitchen and hugged her from behind as she checked the two large pans of lasagna she had just removed from the oven. "I'm sure the guys will appreciate it."

She clasped his hands and squeezed before resuming her work. "You just make sure that everybody who wants a piece gets a piece before Niner and Atlas get at it. Niner can eat his weight and Atlas loves to carbo-load before a mission."

Dawson tossed his head back and laughed as he let go. "You've got those two pegged." He checked his watch and headed for the bathroom. "I'm due at the Unit in an hour."

"Well, make it fast. I intend to let you bang my brains out before you leave."

Dawson headed for the bathroom with a toothy grin. "Your wish is my command."

The Unit

Fort Liberty, North Carolina

Dawson shook his head at Niner and Atlas sitting at the far end of the boardroom table, each with a fork, attacking one of the trays of lasagna, working it from opposite ends. Master Sergeant Mike "Red" Belme, Dawson's second-in-command and best friend, rolled his eyes and stepped over, leaned in, and using a spatula, cut himself a big piece out of the middle before scooping it onto his plate.

"Hey!" protested Niner. "I was going to eat that."

"Not if I got there first," boomed Atlas in his impossibly deep voice. "I need my carbs."

"Tough," replied Red. "Maggie made it for all of us."

Niner stabbed a fork in the air at Dawson. "Next time, I'm reserving a tray."

"Me too," mumbled Atlas through a mouthful of noodles, sauce, and cheese.

"I'll mention it, but you two better save a piece for the colonel. His wife's out of town and he knows this is in the building."

Forks froze all around the table, some in mid-air, as eyes shifted to the empty tray, then to the one Niner and Atlas were working on.

Red sat and cut off a bite-sized chunk then stabbed it, holding up the morsel of lasagna. "All I know is this is mine." He indicated the second tray with his fork. "The colonel's piece is in there."

"Agreed," said Spock, and the feeding frenzy resumed at a brisker pace than moments ago, the only exception Niner and Atlas, who exchanged looks then stared at the tray.

Niner indicated the lasagna still in the center. "If we angle it just right, we can get a good-sized piece out of that."

Atlas shrugged. "Or we eat it all, hide the evidence, and deny knowing anything about it."

"I like how you think."

Dawson cleared his throat and the two men's heads whipped toward him. "You two will be saving a generous piece for your commanding officer. Otherwise, my wife's lasagna will never grace your lips again."

Niner turned to Atlas. "The instant versus delayed gratification debate."

"He's bluffing," said Atlas.

Dawson eyeballed him. "Try me. You know how close Maggie is with the colonel. Pissing me off is one thing, pissing her off is something entirely different."

The door to the briefing room opened and Clancy stepped inside. Niner rose, grabbing the tray and holding it out to him. "We saved you a piece."

Clancy eyed the half-eaten tray. "I can see that." He grabbed a fork from the center of the table, but not one of the paper plates. Instead, he sat and tapped the table in front of him. "Sergeant."

Niner hesitated, though only for a moment, before placing the tray in front of Clancy. Their commanding officer took a bite and moaned before turning to Dawson. "Tell your wife this stuff is like ambrosia, food of the gods."

Niner whimpered and Clancy jabbed the tines of his fork toward Niner and his partner in crime. "You two settle down. I get enough of that from my dogs at home."

"Yes, sir," they both mumbled.

Clancy gestured at the clock. "Let's get started, Sergeant Major."

"Yes, sir," said Dawson, activating the main display. "Gentlemen, we're going to Mexico, and if we're not careful, some of us might not be making it back."

Operations Center 2, CIA Headquarters

Langley, Virginia

CIA Analyst Supervisor Chris Leroux stared at the massive display that arced across the front of the state-of-the-art operations center buried in the bowels of CIA Headquarters in Langley, Virginia. His heart raced as scores of helicopters lifted off, loaded with America's finest, asked yet again to fight another war, this one on their very doorstep against an enemy who had no respect for the rules of combat, nor any concept of honor. They were an inhuman enemy, worse than the Islamic fundamentalists, for at least they were committing their atrocities for a twisted ideology.

The Mexican cartels did it purely for money.

This was the start of the latest and largest operation in the history of America's war on drugs, and as far as he was concerned, it was about damn time. It was clear the Mexicans were either incapable of or unwilling to take care of things within their own borders, and Americans were dying every day because of the poison and the violence that came with it. He liked the Chinese policy when it came to drug dealers. A speedy trial that often lasted only minutes, then a swift execution in public.

Amazingly, their drug problem was nothing compared to America's.

Unfortunately, too much of the Western world had lumped in the dealers with the victims, claiming it was society's fault that they felt it necessary to join gangs and peddle drugs, and kill each other along with innocent bystanders over turf wars. Lots of people grew up poor, but they didn't join gangs. They didn't deal drugs, they didn't shoot their neighbors. They worked their asses off and bettered themselves so that they could have a better life than their parents did, and the next generation could have an even better one.

But today, America was fighting back. If everything went according to plan, the twelve largest drug lords in Mexico would be in custody or dead by morning. Unfortunately, thanks to the president having announced this was happening, the bad guys knew they were coming.

It was one of the reasons things had been delayed two days. The cartels would have been expecting them to come in right away, so would have been on full alert from the moment the announcement was made. By now, they would be sleep deprived, and hopped up on speed or Red Bull. Special Forces had been moved into position in California, Texas, and Florida, with some on carriers positioned in the Pacific and Caribbean off the shores of Mexico, allowing them to execute a coordinated attack, every site to be hit at once.

"Bravo Team just launched," reported his second-in-command, Senior Analyst Sonya Tong.

Leroux rose. "All right, show's over. ETA to target?"

"Twenty-eight minutes."

"Okay, double-check everything. Make sure our satellite coverage is complete, that nothing in the network has gone down since the last check, and double-check our drones. If something is going to go wrong, I don't want it to be on our end. Remember who we're dealing with here. If any of our guys are captured, they'll be tortured to death, and these twisted bastards will make sure the family sees the video."

He turned to the room, filled to capacity with the best in the business, all hands on deck for this massive undertaking, much of it based on CIA intel gathered over months in preparation for this day. "You all have your assignments. Two to a man. Your job is to have eyes on your assigned Bravo Team member at all times. Never take your eyes off them. If someone falls or disappears, you report it immediately so that the information can be passed on. I don't want anyone left behind, but if someone is, I want to know where they are so we can send in an extraction team to get them out before it's too late." He turned to Tong. "Status?"

"Redundant satellite coverage confirmed. We'll have eyes on the target for the entire expected length of the operation plus about an hour after. We can also retask if necessary, should someone be left behind."

"Drones?"

"Both are functioning and can monitor for at least two hours longer if we're willing to let them ditch."

"Understood. And our officer?"

"In position and ready to deploy on our mark."

Leroux checked the clock, everything timed to the second. The digital display flipped to the next minute. "Send the signal."

Álamos, Mexico

CIA Operations Officer Sherrie White smiled. "Acknowledged, Control. Deploying now."

She tapped the keyboard of her laptop and several dozen microdrones, all laid out on a table to her right, lifted off then sped out the open window and into the night. She had been in Álamos for three days now, posing as a college student renting a small house through Airbnb for the week. It had been a pleasant assignment so far, her job singular and easy—get in position, play your part, deploy the drones when ordered, then get the hell out of Dodge.

Once the assault on Salvador Garza's compound was complete, especially if the mission were successful, they expected what remained of his men to swarm the surrounding area searching for people like her, not only because she might have been involved, but because she was American and could be held as a hostage.

It was a prospect she didn't want to risk. After tonight, things would never be the same in Mexico, and perhaps even back home. She had no idea how the cartels would react, though she suspected it would be violent. The briefing she had received before deployment indicated Washington was operating under the assumption the cartels would take a lesson from 9/11 and not repeat Al-Qaeda's mistake—cause too much carnage, and an entire nation and the world could respond. All the senior leadership behind the attack were now dead, and the cartels were not jihadists who believed that when they died spreading their hate, they were rewarded with eternal bliss. Cartel leadership valued their lives.

If they overreacted, they could find themselves on a very long hit list.

She checked her laptop and confirmed all the drones had successfully deployed and were en route to the compound where Garza, the most notorious cartel boss in the country, was holed up. She activated her comms. "Control, Skylark. Confirming successful deployment of drones. Can you confirm on your end, over?"

Tong replied. "Skylark, Control. We can confirm successful deployment. We now have control of the drones through the relay. Recommend you evac now, over."

"Roger that, Control. Heading for evac point Alpha now. Skylark, out." She snapped the laptop shut and stuck it in her bag. She gave the room one final once over, then zipped up the bag and headed out the door with a smile. She couldn't wait to get home to the man she loved.

Chris Leroux, from all outward appearances, was her polar opposite, but there was just something about him that she couldn't resist, and every indication was that this relationship was going the distance. The only thing that would end it would be her untimely death while on an op like this, which was why she set a brisk pace. She wanted to get out of harm's way, but also back into the arms of the man she loved.

And shag him rotten.

Operations Center 2, CIA Headquarters

Langley, Virginia

Leroux stared at the display, a grid of cameras from the drones deployed by Sherrie consuming his attention. Those in the room, assisted by the computer, were identifying targets, displaying their locations on a map of the compound. The place was crawling with hostiles, the computer indicating 47 identified already.

"She's at the train station now," reported Tong.

"ETA to the next train?"

"Nine minutes out."

"Good. Let me know when she's on it." He turned toward Danny Packman, one of their senior analysts. "Any indication the children aren't in their rooms?"

Packman tapped his keyboard then jerked his chin toward the display, two of the images enlarged. "These two drones are just outside their bedrooms." He enhanced the image, switching to infrared, showing the children asleep in their beds.

"Good. Keep a constant eye on them. As soon as the shit hits the fan, they're liable to run to their parents' bedroom. We don't want them getting caught in the crossfire. If any children die tonight, the do-gooders will twist this to make us look like the bad guys."

"Control, Zero-One, status update, over."

Leroux activated his comms, Dawson and his team only five minutes out. "Zero-One, Control Actual. Microdrones are in position. The computer has identified"—he checked the latest count—"fifty-six potential hostiles. Both children are confirmed in their beds." He snapped his fingers, pointing at the display. "Where's our primary?"

Packman pulled up another image. "He and his wife are still in bed."

"Primary target is confirmed in his bed with his wife."

"Understood, Control. Feed the targeting positions to our tactical computers and notify us of any changes with respect to the primary and the children."

"Roger that, Zero-One. We're actively monitoring."

"Copy that, Control. Zero-One, out."

Leroux turned to Tong. "Status on the other missions?"

Tong checked her computer. "Team Seven has aborted. A mechanical problem on their Black Hawk forced them to turn around."

Leroux cursed. "Who were they after?"

"Rebollo."

"Washington's not going to be happy with that. He's one of the ones they're most eager to get their hands on. Everyone else is on target?"

"Yes, sir. So far, so good."

"Let's hope it stays that way." He glanced at the timer counting down to Bravo Team's insertion. Three minutes. The next half-hour would be intense.

He just prayed he wouldn't be attending any funerals when it was over.

Approaching Álamos, Mexico

Dawson stared at his tactical computer's display, strapped to his left forearm, scores of targets highlighted. The number had doubled since yesterday's briefing, making their job much more difficult. He glanced over at Red. "Good thing we brought those autonomous weapons systems with us. As soon as we're in position, make sure the computers paint all the targets, then identify the ones that it can't get a line of sight on so we can take those out manually."

"You got it." Red grinned. "And I'll try to make sure it doesn't paint any of you guys."

"That would be nice," said Niner. "Using a computer to autonomously kill people is way too Terminator-like for me."

Atlas eyed him. "I think you're just afraid to be out of a job."

Niner dismissed the idea. "Nope. The day that I can retire because I'm no longer needed will be the happiest day of my life. But no longer needed because I've been replaced by a computer? Hell no. That means the problem still exists. Peace on Earth, my man. That's the only solution."

"Good luck with that."

Niner grunted. "I know, right? Seems like every day things just keep getting worse. It's been too long since we've had a good world war to remind people just how horrifying it is."

"Yeah, there's a problem with that though. Wasn't it Einstein who said, 'I do not know with what weapons World War III will be fought, but World War IV will be fought with sticks and stones.'?"

"This Einstein character sounds intelligent."

Atlas shrugged. "I don't know about that. He was some sort of patent clerk."

Dawson eyed the two operators. "You two finished?"

Niner gave him a toothy smile. "Are we ever?"

"Sixty seconds!" shouted the pilot from the cockpit.

"Copy that, sixty seconds!" replied Dawson. "Equipment check." It was an unnecessary command, everyone already started. Body armor was inspected, comms and computers tested, everyone giving a thumbs-up. As the door to the Black Hawk slid open, Dawson positioned himself to be first out. The chopper bounced hard, the insertion rapid, and he jumped out then cleared the rotors as the rest of his team followed, spreading out and taking a knee, the chopper lifting off seconds later.

Dawson confirmed their position on his GPS, the Black Hawk crew having inserted them exactly as planned. He took a bearing then pointed. "Ten minutes that way. I want to be in position and set up before the attack helicopters arrive and blow our cover."

Red glanced at the night sky ahead. "I just hope Officer White's distraction covered our insertion."

Dawson stared at the remnants of said distraction ahead. "Let's hope."

Álamos, Mexico

Sherrie suppressed a smile as those around her waiting for the train to arrive ooh'd and aah'd at the fireworks display that had just ended. She had set it up earlier in the day, inside the courtyard of the small home she had rented. It was designed to last for three minutes, and was triggered by Langley. The moment the chopper approached, the whistles, pops, and explosions should have been enough to not only distract the guards at the compound, but cover the sound of the rotors of the massive Black Hawk as it delivered Bravo Team into position.

The whistle of the train had everyone returning their attention to the track. She spotted the light on the engine rounding the bend and her heart picked up a few beats. The attack on the compound would begin in less than ten minutes, and assuming the train departed on schedule, she should be far enough away to avoid any problems. If everything continued to go to plan, she would get off at the next stop where a car would be waiting for her with a CIA asset that would bring her to Obregón, where she would catch a plane home.

Fingers crossed.

Approaching Garza Residence

Outside Álamos, Mexico

Dawson pointed to his right and Sergeant Gerry "Jimmy Olsen" Hudson broke off with Sergeant Eugene "Jagger" Thomas, lugging one of the automated weapon systems. They continued toward the compound, well-lit ahead, then he pointed to the left, sending Sergeants Danny "Casey" Martin and Trip "Mickey" McDonald to set up the second of three automated systems, Red along with three other team members having already split off to set up the final position at the rear. They would have coverage from three angles that should allow them to eliminate most of the targets in the initial assault, but nothing would be triggered until they were detected.

He activated his comms. "Control, Zero-One, start dimming the lights, over."

"Roger that, Zero-One. Beginning to dim the lights."

Dawson and the remainder of the team continued toward the compound. Niner came up beside him, staring ahead at the bright lights flooding their target. "Is it working? I can't tell."

"That's the whole idea. They're not supposed to be able to tell. Langley is slowly dropping the strength of the power being sent into the compound. As long as they do it gradually enough, nobody will notice, and in the next few minutes, those that are outside will barely have any light left, and those inside should start to have equipment failures. When they do notice, they should think it's a problem at the power station and not a prelude to an attack."

"I like it," pronounced Niner. "What will these CIA guys come up with next?"

Red's voice cut in over the comms and Dawson smiled, his friend out of breath. "Zero-One, Zero-Two, we're in position, over."

"Copy that, Zero-Two." Dawson pointed at a stone formation ahead and they all slowed up. "We're in position as well. Zero-One to Bravo Team, notify me as each of your systems are set up, over."

Casey responded first. "Zero-One, Zero-Four, position number one is up and ready. Confirmed synced with Control, over."

"Copy that, Zero-Four,"

Jimmy reported in next. "Zero-One, One-Zero, position number two is set up, synced with Control and acquiring targets, over."

"Copy that, One-Zero."

Sergeant Zach "Wings" Hauser, who had headed for the rear of the compound with Red but would be manning the weapon system, was the last to report. "Zero-One, One-Two, weapon system is online, synced with Control and acquiring targets, over."

"Copy that, One-Two." Dawson took a knee. "Control, Zero-One, all three weapon systems are reported synced and ready. Can you confirm, over?"

Leroux replied. "Zero-One, Control Actual, syncing of all three weapon systems confirmed, targets are being fed to the computers. We'll be ready to go in less than sixty seconds, over."

"Status on the priority targets?"

"Primary is still in bed with his wife. Children are still in their separate beds."

Dawson peered through his binoculars, Niner, Atlas, and Spock doing the same. He pointed left of the main entrance. "The blind spot Langley identified is twenty meters to the left of the gate." He indicated a depression fifty yards ahead, the long shadows cast by the dimming lights growing less distinct with each passing moment. "Let's go." He rose and sprinted toward the depression, the others on his heels. He hit the ground, Niner and Spock on either side of him, the lumbering Atlas half a dozen paces behind.

Niner glanced at his friend. "I told you, you ate too much lasagna."

"You ate just as much as me."

"Yeah, but I'm svelte. You're already slow."

"I may be slower than you, but I can maintain the same speed carrying six of you."

Niner eyed him. "Has that ever proven useful?"

"You better hope we never have to find out."

The lights ahead flickered. Dawson checked left toward the village where Sherrie had been staying and found the lights failing there as well. "Control, Zero-One, lights are flickering here. Any indication they're concerned?"

"Zero-One, Control. Negative. We've been doing this for the past week. Ramp it down, ramp it up. They should interpret it as normal problems at the power plant. No indication that they're expecting anything, over."

Dawson and the others exchanged smiles. "Copy that, Control. Are we clear to proceed?"

"Stand by, Zero-One. We're waiting for Team Eleven to get into position. Estimated ninety seconds to synchronized attack, over."

"Copy that, Control. Ninety seconds. Standing by for your order to proceed, over." Dawson turned to the others. "Ninety seconds. As soon as we're given the order, we'll get to the wall, go over, then attempt to extract the primary without being detected. If we're really lucky, we might get in and out without anyone noticing."

Niner groaned. "When are we ever lucky?"

Atlas gave Niner a look. "You're finally dating. Shouldn't you be getting lucky all the time now?"

Niner grinned. "Well, if we're talking that kinda lucky, I've lost count."

"That's just because you're using your fingers and toes."

Niner's eyes shot wide. "You can use your toes?"

Atlas groaned and Spock snickered when their comms squawked.

"This is Commander Operation Striking Dagger to all teams. You are clear to proceed. I repeat, you are clear to proceed, over."

Dawson responded, as did the other dozen team leads. "Bravo Leader acknowledges, proceeding with mission, over."

The lights to the compound flickered out and everyone rose, sprinting toward the wall. Niner and Spock reached it first, Spock dropping to his hands and knees. Dawson sprinted toward him then launched himself off the ground, pressing a boot into Spock's back as he reached for the top of the wall. His cut-resistant gloves grasped the barbed wire at the top and he pulled himself up and over, straddling the wall. Reaching down, he pulled Atlas up as Niner pushed on the big man's free foot. Atlas flipped over and back down to the ground on the other side as Dawson hauled Niner up then Spock, before dropping to the ground himself. The lights flickered back on, Langley monitoring their progress, coordinating everything like it was a symphony.

The lights were quite dim now, blinking occasionally, Langley's manipulation of the grid masterful. Dawson quickly scanned the area, picking out over half a dozen guards, none looking in his direction, most staring up at the uncooperative lights. He rushed after the others using a line of bushes for cover.

"Zero-One, drop." It was Leroux's voice in his ear.

He hit the deck without questioning why. Two guards rounded the corner of the main structure, approaching his position and that of the others huddled at the far end of the hedgerow. All it would take would be for one of them to glance to their left as they passed. He drew his Glock and screwed in the suppressor, then using hand signals, delivered his orders to the others. Spock readied his own Glock as Niner and Atlas set aside their MP5s and drew their knives.

The two guards approached and Leroux updated him. "After you take out these two, you should be clear. Signal when you want us to cut the lights."

The audio would be fed only to those affected by what was going on. There was no need to confuse the rest of the team with a situation they weren't necessarily aware of. "Now," he murmured.

The lights flickered again then the compound fell dark. Dawson watched as Niner and Atlas leaped to their feet, grabbing the unsuspecting guards and covering their mouths with one hand while slitting their throats with the other. Expert, precise, and swift, both bodies dragged behind the hedgerow within moments of the attack beginning.

The lights came back on as Dawson joined the others. "Good work. Let's get inside before these two are missed." He pointed at an open window on the second level to their far left. "That's his room." He activated his comms. "Control, Zero-One. What's the status on our target?"

"Zero-One, Control. Still asleep. His wife woke briefly during the fireworks. She appears to be back asleep. Children are still asleep in their rooms."

"Copy that, Control. Bravo Team, Zero-One. We're attempting entry now, over."

The various sub-units acknowledged.

"Control, Zero-One, confirm we're clear, over."

"Zero-One, Control. All guards are still stationary except for two roving patrols that are on the opposite side of the building. For the moment, you're clear to go."

"Copy that. Kill the lights."

The compound fell dark yet again and the four of them raced for the window. Niner slung his MP5 and leaped at the wall, an architectural element jutting out from the main building giving him a 90-degree angle to work with. His left foot pressed into the stucco, giving him leverage and momentum to jump several more feet, his right foot gripping the main wall as he reached up and grabbed a drainage pipe, quickly scaling to the second floor and the open window.

"Control, status," said Dawson.

"Primary and his wife are still asleep. No indication they heard him."

Dawson gave Niner a thumbs-up and the operator hooked a rope from his belt over the windowsill. He gave it a good tug then tossed it down to the ground. Dawson grabbed it and hung from it for a moment, confirming it was secure, then rapidly scaled the wall, watching as Niner above him stealthily entered the bedroom. Dawson reached the top and quietly climbed over the window ledge. The moment his foot was on the bedroom floor the rope tensed again as Spock followed.

Dawson withdrew a small spray bottle from one of his many pockets, Niner doing the same. They approached opposite sides of the bed as Spock entered behind them, drawing his Glock and screwing on the suppressor, covering them. Dawson extended his hand, his finger on the top of the pump, aiming it at their target's face as Niner did the same to the wife. Niner gave him a nod and Dawson returned it, pressing down on the pump twice. His target flinched, his eyes shooting wide, his mouth opening with a gasp that sealed his fate, the involuntary reaction causing him to inhale the fumes. The man's eyes fluttered before he slumped, out cold.

Dawson glanced over at Niner as the man checked the wife's pulse. "She's fine, out cold," he whispered.

"Good. Let's get this guy the hell out of here." Dawson tossed the sheet aside and frowned at the naked body underneath.

Niner grinned. "I'm glad he's going over your shoulder and not mine."

Dawson grabbed the man under the armpits and hauled him up, tossing him over his shoulder and heading for the window.

Leroux's voice piped in. "Zero-One, Control. It looks like the locals are getting restless. We've got to get these lights back on, over."

"Working on it," replied Dawson.

Spock fit a harness over their unconscious target's body then attached it to the rope. Dawson shoved him out the window and he dropped quickly toward the ground and into Atlas' arms.

"Let's go."

Spock flipped over the window then dropped, Niner following. Dawson did one last check of the room then climbed over the edge, unhooking the rope and dropping it to the ground below. He hopped over to the drainage pipe and scurried down to the ground where he found Niner coiling the rope and Atlas with their target slung over his shoulder, as if he were nothing more than a sack of potatoes.

Somebody shouted to their right and Dawson cursed.

"Zero-One, Control. You've been spotted, over."

"Copy that, Control. Zero-One to Bravo Team. Light them up, and let's hope that damn AI recognizes friendlies."

Acknowledgments from the three automated sniper teams came in over his earpiece as the lethal automated weapons systems opened up on the compound. Dawson and the others sprinted toward the outer wall, covering Atlas as he lumbered with his heavy load like a juggernaut. All around them, weapons fired blindly from an enemy taken completely by surprise, the computers controlling the three automated gun placements firing two rapid rounds at each target they had been tracking. Anybody within their sights would be taken out within seconds. The problem would be those inside, currently hidden from the targeting systems.

They reached the wall unscathed. Spock boosted Dawson to the top. Dawson extended an arm and pulled Spock up with him as Atlas heaved their target toward them. They each grabbed an arm and dragged him up then flipped him over onto the ground, the man smacking onto the unforgiving dirt with an unceremonious thud. They both reached down and hauled Atlas up as Niner pushed from below, the big man expertly flipping over the wall and dropping on the other side, sticking the landing. Dawson helped Niner up and the agile warrior cleared the wall and landed beside his friend, who already had their prisoner over his shoulder once again.

Gunfire sprayed the wall and Spock took a round to the back. Gasping from the impact, he fell off the top of the wall and onto the ground below as Dawson took two to the chest, his body shaking with each impact. Unfortunately, unlike Spock, he fell inside the compound.

He gulped for breath, checking his chest and finding two bullets embedded in his armor.

He would survive, but heavy footfalls rapidly approached, perhaps sealing his fate.

A head poked out from above. "Come on, BD, we don't have time for this shit," chastised Niner in a mocking tone.

Dawson pushed to his elbows as more gunfire sprayed the wall, narrowly missing Niner, and Clancy's words echoed.

Don't allow yourself to be taken prisoner.

He rose to his knees, unslinging his MP5 as he opened fire on the approaching enemy. Niner joined in from above.

"RPG!" warned Leroux in his ear.

Dawson hit the ground as the rocket-propelled grenade streaked toward their position, slamming into the wall. Niner yelped as he dropped to the ground on the other side.

"One-One, Zero-One, status?"

"I'm fine," replied Niner.

Dawson continued to fire, now prone, but it was clear he couldn't hold out for long. "Bravo Team, Zero-One, complete the mission. Zero-One, out." He deactivated his comms to put a stop to any protests, and continued to fire his MP5, reloading with his last mag as the automated weapons systems continued to pour fire on the compound. Unfortunately, too many of the enemy were using the outer wall as cover now that they realized where the weapons fire was coming from.

He didn't have to hold out for too long. The moment they had been discovered, two Apache gunships, holding to the north, would have been dispatched once the element of surprise had been lost and their rotors would give nothing away. If he could hold out, they could provide him the distraction to get over that wall and join the others. He continued his disciplined rounds, the bodies of his enemy littering the ground. He reactivated his comms and heard Red barking orders now that he was in command.

Leroux noticed he was back online. "Zero-One, Control, status."

"I'm still alive if that's what you're wondering."

"Apaches are inbound. ETA thirty seconds. Can you hold that long?"

"As long as they don't get a lucky shot off, I should be good. Status on the target?"

"Your team is clear of the compound and heading for the extraction point. Black Hawk is inbound. ETA sixty seconds."

"Just make sure everybody—"

Somebody said something in the background. "Stand by, Zero-One." Leroux cursed. "Zero-One, we've got reinforcements coming in from the town. Six vehicles. It looks like they had some sort of emergency response team set up."

"ETA?"

"Two minutes."

"Instruct Zero-Two to proceed on mission. I want everybody on that Black Hawk and out of here. Don't worry about me."

"Understood, Zero-One, relaying order."

Sonya Tong's voice cut in, the order being relayed to the others, a swift string of dissension filling his ears. He cursed as his chest tightened.

"Bravo Team, Zero-One, you have your orders. Extract now then plan a rescue mission, but only if it's feasible. I don't want anybody dying to save my sorry ass."

Red acknowledged the order. "Roger that, Zero-One, proceeding with mission. Good luck."

Niner cut in. "I'll be back for you. I promise you that."

Dawson smiled as he fired his last round from the MP5 and switched to his Glock. He squeezed off two rounds. "Red, if I don't make it, take care of Maggie."

"The Unit takes care of its own. You don't have to worry about her."

He fired two more rounds, taking out another target, but there were just too many, and the automated systems had been packed up because they couldn't be left behind, the technology far too valuable. A round hammered into his back, closer this time, and he grunted as he slammed onto the ground, his Glock dropping to his side. He wouldn't last until the choppers got here, even though he could hear their rotors thundering in the distance.

"This is it, boys, it's been an honor. Tell Maggie that I love her, and that my final thoughts were of her."

Silence was the response before Red, the best friend he had ever had, finally replied, his voice subdued. "The honor has been ours, and I'll deliver your final message personally, old friend."

Footfalls surrounded him, orders shouted in Spanish and English. He flipped over onto his back and stared up into the muzzle of an assault rifle.

"Any final words, gringo?"

Dawson smiled. "Yeah, bring the rain."

Operations Center 2, CIA Headquarters

Langley, Virginia

Leroux watched in horror as the Apaches opened fire, rockets laying waste to much of the compound, though the main residential portion was left untouched to protect the children inside. He spun toward Marc Therrien, responsible for Dawson. "Whatever you do, don't lose contact with him."

"I've still got him. His vitals are still coming in strong. He's still alive, somehow."

Leroux turned to Tong. "Notify command to have the combat search and rescue team deployed immediately."

"I'm on it," she replied.

Red's voice came in over the speakers. "Control, Zero-Two. Target is secure, eleven members of the team on board. Zero-One presumed in enemy hands. We're lifting off now, over."

"Acknowledged, Zero-Two. Apaches are engaging hostiles now. We'll keep you updated on Zero-One's status. Control, out." He faced

Packman. "Let me know the moment Bravo Team has left Mexican airspace."

"Yes, sir."

He turned to Tong. "ETA on that rescue team?"

"Twelve minutes."

He cursed. "Twelve minutes might as well be twelve days."

Approaching Garza Residence

Outside Álamos, Mexico

Sherrie hammered on the accelerator as she raced the beater she had stolen toward the compound and Dawson's last reported position. The train had been delayed in leaving, and the moment she had heard Dawson was down, she had sprung into action, rushing off the station platform and commandeering the first car she could find.

Explosions and tracer fire lit the night sky ahead, the compound sitting atop a hill like a castle of old now a shadow of its former self, walls crumbling, buildings afire. There was no way Dawson was surviving this. No one was surviving this.

She had heard his final words. "Bring the rain." It was him sealing his own fate while ensuring maximum enemy casualties. He knew he was going to die, so he gave the Apache crews an out.

One of the gunships banked toward her position, its guns spitting death on the ground below. Multiple explosions indicated the gunner sitting in the front seat had succeeded in hitting his targets, and she realized it must have been the reinforcements Leroux had referred to.

She gulped and activated her comms. "Control, Skylark, friendly approaching on the village road. I'm in a white Toyota Corolla, over." She could almost hear Leroux cursing.

"Skylark, Control Actual. Flash your lights, over."

She did as told and had to assume the information was being relayed to the Apaches. The attacking chopper veered off, ending its approach and returning to the compound.

"Skylark, Control Actual, you're cleared. State your intentions, over."

Her boyfriend wasn't happy, and the only reason she wasn't getting chewed out over the air was because of their relationship. "I was still in theater when Zero-One was reported down. I can get him. Just guide me in."

There was a pause. "Transferring you," was the curt reply, then Marc Therrien came on the line.

"Skylark, Control. I've still got vitals on him. He appears to be against the front wall where they made entry."

She rounded the bend, the compound just ahead, the lights that normally lit it dead, though she could see everything clearly from the fires and the constant muzzle flashes. "Notify those gunships of my location and my intention to enter. I don't mind dying for my country, but I'd really hate it if it was my country that did the killing."

Garza Residence

Outside Álamos, Mexico

The moment the Apaches had opened fire, Dawson's captors had gone into survival mode, scrambling for cover and directing their attention toward the gunships. He had taken the opportunity to roll toward the wall and was now pressed up against it, his hands clasped over his head, a useless gesture since a single round from the Apache's 30 millimeter chain gun would slice through him like a plasma torch.

A rocket slammed into the wall not five feet from his position, the stone crumbling into a pile. Somebody shouted something, the word 'stinger' all he could make out. He cursed and activated his comms. "Control, Zero-One, hostiles may have Stingers. Order the pilots to break off their attack, over." He grabbed an M82 semi-automatic rifle off a body lying beside him, then scanned the area, spotting no one with a shoulder-launched missile system. The Apaches broke off when he heard a yell. He pushed to a knee and opened fire, taking out a two-man team about to launch from the roof.

Shouts from his greatly thinned-out enemy around him had him spraying the area with what was left of the magazine before he tossed the weapon aside and dove through the hole in the wall. A car skidded to a halt nearby and he cursed as he realized it had to be the reinforcements Langley had referred to.

A familiar face poked out the window. "You waiting for an engraved invitation? Get the hell in!" ordered Sherrie White, a CIA operations officer he had worked with on several occasions.

He stumbled toward the passenger side and climbed in, the front wheels already spinning before he could close the door.

"Control, Skylark. I've got him, repeat, I've got Zero-One!"

"Copy that, Skylark," replied Leroux, and she could hear the elation in his voice. "Report to extraction point Charlie. Search and rescue team will rendezvous with you there, over."

"Copy that. Heading for rendezvous point Charlie. Skylark, out." She turned to Dawson. "You okay?"

He shrugged and winced. "I took a few rounds to the vest. I'll be bruised up, but I should be good to go in a few days." He held up a finger and activated his comms. "Zero-One, Control, you make sure that everybody at Bragg and on Bravo Team knows my status. I'd really hate for the funeral plans to go too far, over."

Leroux chuckled in his ear. "Copy that, Zero-One. We'll make sure everyone knows you're still alive and kicking."

"Good. And pass on my thanks to those Apache crews. They saved this grunt."

"Will do, Zero-One."

Dawson leaned back and closed his eyes as Sherrie guided them down the hill, and he said a silent prayer of thanks. The gods of war had been on his side.

Nobody from Bravo Team was getting skinned alive tonight.

Garza Residence

Outside Álamos, Mexico

Juan Garza stepped out of the back of his SUV and onto the cobblestone courtyard of his brother's home, the place he had visited hundreds of times over the years now barely recognizable. Bodies were still being piled, the wounded already rushed to nearby hospitals. But he didn't care about the minions.

All he cared about was his family.

His brother's wife, Maria, cried out and rushed toward him, her tear-stained cheeks clear evidence of how distraught the woman was. She collapsed into his arms and he held her tight as his young niece and nephew ran toward him, their arms outstretched, wailing their terror.

"Are you all right?" he asked, holding Maria out and inspecting her for any wounds before doing the same with both of the children.

"We're fine. They didn't touch us. I don't know what happened. I was asleep and then when I woke up, it was all over." She gripped her temples. "I have a splitting headache."

"Were you drinking?"

She shook her head. "Just a glass of wine at dinner. Could they have drugged me?"

"They must have. They definitely would've had to drug Salvador. There's no way he went with them willingly or without putting up a fight."

"What happened? Who was it?"

He frowned. "It had to be Americans. They said they were coming, but I don't think any of us actually believed they'd do it."

"El Jefe?"

Garza turned toward one of his brother's guards, hailing him from the doorway. "There's something on the TV you're going to want to see."

"I'll be there in a minute." He turned to Maria. "Pack up what you'll need. You and the children will be staying with me until we get this sorted out."

Maria placed a hand on his cheek, staring into his eyes. "Thank you. I know this puts you in charge now, but please, do whatever you can to get my husband back."

He pressed his hand on hers. "Trust me. I'll do everything I can to get him back, and if I can't, I'll make sure the Americans pay a price so heavy, they'll never again think of interfering in our business."

Fort Cavazos, formerly Fort Hood

Outside Killeen, Texas

Dawson smiled as Red entered the infirmary.

"What's the verdict?" asked his friend.

Dawson shrugged. "I'm still breathing, so in my inexpert opinion, I'm still alive."

"I figured that much out for myself. The question is, are you going to remain that way?"

A doctor at a nearby bed stepped over and glanced at the monitors. "Any other mere mortal would probably be begging for death right now, but your friend has a remarkable tolerance for pain. He'll be fine. Just a little tender for a few days."

"How are his ribs?"

"Good. Amazingly, he didn't even crack anything."

"Am I cleared for duty?"

"Light duty. Report back here tomorrow morning. We just want to make sure we didn't miss anything, but my guess is you'll be medically cleared for active duty in a couple of days."

Dawson smiled. "Good enough for me. Can I go?"

"Yep."

Dawson reached out to yank off all the cables attached to him when the doctor eyeballed him. "How about we let a nurse take care of that very expensive equipment?"

Dawson smiled sheepishly. "Sorry about that, Doc. I guess I've been watching too many movies."

"Nurse, can you take care of him for me?"

The young man nodded. "Sure thing, Doctor."

Red stepped back as Dawson held out his arms, all the leads removed along with his IV. "Where are my clothes?"

The nurse chuckled. "There wasn't much left of them by the time you got here."

Red held up a bag that so far had gone unnoticed. "I brought you something to wear."

"Who picked them out?"

"I did."

Dawson sighed in relief. "Thank God. I was afraid Niner put together something."

"If he heard you say that, he'd be crushed, so I'll be certain to let him know."

Dawson laughed as he dressed. "How's Spock?"

"He's fine. Just a little bruise. He's already been cleared for active duty. Everyone else is fine. Just a few bumps and scrapes."

"And the overall operation?"

"Eleven of twelve were successful. One was aborted due to equipment failure."

Dawson whistled as he buttoned up his shirt. "Eleven of twelve. Holy shit, that's way better than I was expecting."

"I think it was way better than anyone was expecting." Red lowered his voice. "I'm afraid we overachieved on this one."

"Any blowback yet?"

"Not much. There's been some random shootings across the country, but that could just be an average Tuesday."

"Yeah, sometimes I wonder why we bother reporting on this stuff anymore. It's clear as a society we've decided human life is worthless."

Red grunted. "Then why even bother doing what we're doing?"

Dawson checked his fly then headed for the door. "Because maybe one day America will wake up, and when it does, it would be nice if there was a country there to save that still flew the Stars and Stripes."

They stepped into the corridor and Red indicated the way. "Well, as long as you're willing to fight, so am I. And speaking of, the colonel wants to talk to you."

"He probably wants to know if there's some Mexican cartel member out there wearing a Dawson skin suit."

"Huh?"

"Nothing. Just something he said in my last one-on-one with him."

Red eyed him. "You two have an odd relationship for a senior officer and a non-comm."

Dawson laughed. "Yeah, and it's gotten even worse since I married Maggie. I think he thinks of her as a daughter, and until we got married, I was just the guy shtupping her. But now that we're married, I get the impression he's more concerned about my safety."

"So, what? This is a father-in-law/son-in-law type relationship?"

"I have no idea. I hope not. I wouldn't want you and the others to get jealous."

Red showed him into a secure comms room and within minutes Dawson was in a video call with Clancy.

"Good to see you're in one piece, Sergeant Major."

"Thank you, sir. They tenderized me a little bit, but those Apaches arrived just in time to save me from becoming the main course at their next fiesta."

Clancy chuckled. "It sounds like they didn't improve your sense of humor."

Dawson shrugged. "All a matter of perspective, sir."

Clancy grunted. "Well, whatever you do, just don't turn into Niner. One of him is enough."

"I'll agree with you there, sir."

Clancy became serious. "Be honest with me. What's your condition?"

Dawson had to be careful. Saying the wrong thing could have him and his team benched for a couple of weeks, but if he lied and said he was good to go, he could be sent on a mission tonight that could put the lives of his team in jeopardy because he wasn't up to snuff. "A little tender, nothing broken, nothing sprained. I'd be confident to deploy in two or three days."

"And Spock?"

"I understand he took a round in the body armor. I haven't spoken to him yet, but apparently he's been cleared."

"Good. We're starting to see some reaction from the cartels. The president wants everybody ready just in case things get ugly."

Dawson's eyes narrowed. "Do you mean deployment within the US, suspension of Posse Comitatus?"

"No. I mean the president's kill list could be about to get dramatically longer if the reports I'm reading from the FBI and the CIA are accurate."

Dawson tensed. "What are you talking about?"

"There was sporadic violence overnight that was ramping up then suddenly stopped. Chatter is suggesting something big tonight, something coordinated. We don't know what yet, but this is what we warned them could happen. If it does, this war we just started could be on the streets of America tonight, and God only knows when it will end."

Dawson frowned, his heart pounding a little harder than when he had entered the room. "Our families?"

"We're not allowed to warn anybody. If the public found out we protected our own, it'd be a PR disaster. I have, however, asked Maggie to work the night shift, and the White House has issued a warning of potential retaliation and has advised citizens to stay indoors after dark and to remain vigilant."

Dawson frowned. "With half of America huddled behind locked doors with a gun in their hand, we're liable to kill more of our own than the criminals are."

"Agreed, Sergeant Major. I would not want to be a delivery boy tonight. Get your rest. I have a funny feeling you and your team are going to be back in it before you know it."

"Yes, sir. And thank you, sir."

"For what?"

"For making Maggie work overtime."

Clancy smirked. "I'd put them all on the payroll if I could. Clancy, out." He leaned forward and ended the call, and Dawson sat for a moment in silence. Maggie would be safe on the base. Some of the men with families were in married quarters, but others lived off-base in the civilian community.

The question was, if the cartel planned to retaliate, would it be against America in general, or would they target the Special Forces that had attacked them? He suspected they would go after the civilian population. Random acts of violence were easy and low risk. It was why terrorism was so effective in disrupting people's lives. Attempting to attack a place like Bragg would be suicide. No, tonight, if blood were to be shed in the name of vengeance, it would be the people of America that would pay the price, then people like him would be unleashed in response.

But to what end? Last night's actions, he feared, had merely triggered a never-ending cycle of retaliatory attacks that would bring the carnage the Mexican population had been suffering, to the streets of America.

Exactly what the Pentagon had feared.

The Unit

Fort Liberty, North Carolina

"I'll talk to him right away. Don't move."

Maggie hung up the phone and leaped from her chair, rushing to Clancy's inner office door that had remained closed since she had reported for duty. She knocked, her raps urgent, unable to hide the fear that threatened to consume her.

"Come!"

She opened the door and stepped inside.

"What is it?"

He looked stressed, tired, the TV on his wall tuned to CNN, the volume low, the horrors playing out across the country on full display. The cartels had retaliated all right, in the bloodiest way imaginable. Hundreds, if not thousands of their foot soldiers spread across every city and town in the country had begun killing random civilians. One or two at a time, five or ten if they had the opportunity. But unlike the crazed gunmen that made the news cycle almost every night in America, they didn't stick around to get shot by the authorities. They weren't trying to get themselves killed in a blaze of glory. They simply moved on to the next opportunity.

Hundreds were dead already, hundreds more wounded, the toll so high, CNN had taken to putting a confirmed body count ticker on the righthand side of their screen. It was disgusting. It was treating the victims like a video game, and one guest had already called them out on it, saying that displaying that number merely encouraged the cartels to force it higher.

"It's Vanessa, sir, Atlas' girlfriend. She's at the main gate and they won't let her in. They've sealed the base. Only authorized personnel and their spouses are allowed in. But it's Vanessa, sir. She might as well be family."

"Where's she going?"

"Red's house. All the families from off-base are heading there. Everyone's terrified."

Clancy closed his eyes for a moment, pinching the bridge of his nose, then sighed. "Is she alone?"

"Yes."

"Okay." He picked up his phone and dialed, then jerked his chin toward the door. "Get me a complete list of all the girlfriends, boyfriends, and children that might be coming in. I'll get them added to the list at the main gate."

"Yes, sir."

Clancy glanced at the screen and cursed, and Maggie turned, her jaw dropping at the chyron on the bottom of the screen.

Over 1000 confirmed dead.

Tears filled her eyes and Clancy pointed at the door. "Get me that list. There's no time to waste."

She hurried out of his office, closing the door behind her as she burst into tears. Her country was being destroyed from within, and the man she loved had been forced to pull the trigger that had caused it.

Garza Cartel Compound

Somewhere in the Sierra Madre Occidental Mountains, Mexico

Juan Garza sat at his desk, buried deep in the side of a cliff face in the Sierra Madre Occidental Mountains, the complex built years ago for just such an occasion. A handful of people knew where it was. Everyone who worked here lived here. If they had to leave, they were blindfolded and taken through multiple checkpoints where drivers were swapped who only knew their portion of the route. Nobody knew he was here, and nobody knew where here was.

Especially the Americans.

This would be where his brother would have coordinated things had he not been taken. But now it was his job. He was El Jefe, in charge of the most powerful cartel in Mexico. They controlled the most territory, had the most men, and moved the most product by far. And while the others were rivals, the call he had put out for unity yesterday morning had been heeded.

All the affected cartels had agreed to coordinate their retaliation. It had been gloriously effective, and the greatest nation on earth now trembled in fear, the confirmed death toll higher than that of 9/11, last night's terror far more debilitating since there wasn't a corner of America that hadn't felt his wrath.

But now it was over. The instructions had been clear. The violence stopped at 6:00 AM this morning, local time, and the orgy of blood had indeed stopped like a switch had been thrown. It was essential that it did, for it indicated it was a controlled event. He had posted a video at 3:00 AM Eastern on social media indicating what was happening, why it was happening, when it would stop, and when it would start again if their demands weren't met.

The immediate release of all eleven taken illegally by the American military.

There was a tap at the door.

"Come in."

It opened, and his sister-in-law Maria entered, her eyes wide, her nostrils flared. There was no fear—it was merely rage. She had sat with him and the others watching the live broadcasts of the carnage, cheering it on, damning the Americans, damning their leaders, damning their military. She had snapped, and he wondered if she would ever recover.

She was so consumed with rage and hatred she was losing herself. She had lost sight of the fact that this was a job. He had nothing against the people of America. They were his customers, after all. The American government, their law enforcement agencies, their military, were merely rivals like any other. It wasn't personal. It was business. What he had ordered last night, the carnage that ensued, the innocent lives lost, wasn't just an act of vengeance, it was a negotiating tactic. Blood was spilled, a demand was made. And should it be met, the fight would be over. But if it wasn't, then it would continue until the Americans returned those they had taken.

"What can I do for you, Maria?"

"Have you heard anything from those bastards?"

He motioned at a chair in front of his desk. "No. Nor do I expect to. Tonight, we'll be targeting our own politicians, police, military leaders, anyone who allowed the Americans to cross into our soil unchallenged."

She sat, her fingers drumming on the wooden arms. "I think I might have a better idea."

He cocked an eyebrow. "Oh?"

She leaned forward. "I think I have a way to use their own arrogance against them, and ensure every demand we want is met."

"And what's that?"

And when she told him, he collapsed back in his seat, staring at the television screen, a smile slowly spreading. The idea was as crazy as the woman who had come up with it, but it was also brilliant. And she was right. If they succeeded, every demand and more would be granted.

Victory would be theirs.

Fort Cavazos

Outside Killeen, Texas

It was being called the Night of Reckoning. The death toll continued to climb as those wounded during the violence succumbed to their injuries, and more bodies were found in the alleyways of America. The orgy of violence unleashed upon an unsuspecting and unprepared nation had brought the country to its knees. Two days had passed, the violence of that one night so far going unrepeated, crime in general down as citizens huddled in their homes, a curfew in place in most of the major cities, police and national guard out in full force, an administration under siege for what every expert, even those previously calling for Washington to do exactly what it had done, now calling it a foolish and rash action.

The question was, why had the cartels stopped? They had made their demands, Washington had refused, declaring they wouldn't negotiate with terrorists, and the arraignments and bail hearings were proceeding as they normally would, bail denied in all cases so far.

"What do you think?" asked Red.

Dawson shook his head as his entire team, gathered in front of the television in one of the rec rooms at the newly renamed Fort Cavazos outside Killeen, Texas, turned to hear what he had to say. "I think this is the calm before the storm."

Spock cocked an eyebrow. "If what happened two nights ago wasn't the storm, I'd hate to see what is."

Dawson drew a breath, holding it for a moment. "That was the cartels demonstrating what they're capable of and showing Washington how disciplined they are. All the attacks stopped at exactly 6:00 AM local, just like they said they would. That means they have complete control over the gangs that operate on our streets, and they can activate them again in a heartbeat. The fact they haven't tells me they've got something else up their sleeve."

"Something worse?" asked Niner.

"Worse or bigger." Dawson gestured toward the screen as a new report came on, the chyron causing heads to shake around the room.

Three Amigos Summit to Proceed.

Dawson jabbed a finger at the screen. "If I were the cartels, that's what I'd be targeting."

Red frowned. "Surely Washington knows how dangerous it would be to hold that thing in Mexico City."

"Welcome to the new Washington. Same as the old. Everyone there knows that if you don't tell your superiors what they want to hear, they'll keep replacing you until they find someone who does. We warned them what could happen and they ignored us, and I have no doubt somebody there warned them that going to Mexico City is idiocy."

Atlas grunted. "I guess now we know why we're on standby."

Dawson rose then turned to Red. "Start putting together equipment lists for our most likely scenarios. I'm going to go talk to the colonel and see what he has to say about this."

Red looked up at him. "Do you think he'll tell you anything?"

Dawson grinned. "Of course he will. I married his daughter."

Garza Cartel Compound

Somewhere in the Sierra Madre Occidental Mountains, Mexico

Garza sat at the head of the boardroom table, the far wall a checkerboard of who was who in the Mexican cartels, or at least who was who now. He had encountered heavy resistance to his plan to halt the attacks, but after he had explained his new plan, most had eagerly agreed, the rest eventually won over reluctantly.

It was high-risk. Extremely high-risk. If they failed, the cost could be dramatic, but if they succeeded, they could get everything they wanted and more.

"The army has moved two entire divisions into the city. Security's never been tighter," said Osiel Trevino, one of the more reluctant family heads.

Garza wagged a finger. "You're mistaken. The army is *moving* two full divisions into the city. They haven't moved them yet. We've already moved weapons and ammo inside, including RPGs, Stingers, and heavy machine guns within the security perimeter that they're just setting up now. We've had trucks going non-stop for two days. The hard part's done. We just need to get our foot soldiers in there then wait for those arrogant fools to hold their meeting."

"And what if we fail?"

"It depends on what your definition of failure is. No matter what happens, there will be chaos in Mexico City. Hundreds of our opponents will be eliminated. And remember, we control the message. If we succeed, then that was our goal. If we fail, then whatever we did accomplish was our goal. When this is over, the public and those who would oppose us will believe we achieved our goals no matter what happens, and they won't dare oppose us again. If we fail and merely kill a bunch of police, the Americans aren't going to release our people. They don't care what happens to people who aren't white. But if they don't set them free, then what they're calling the Night of Reckoning will become the week of and the month of. Innocent blood will fill the gutters of the streets of America until we get what we want. Trust me, my friends, our family heads will be returned to us either next week with the success of our Mexico City operation, or within a few weeks after tens of thousands are dead and the American public demands their government give in."

"You seem to have a lot of confidence in your plan."

Garza smiled. "I do, because I have an ace up my sleeve that even the Americans won't be expecting."

Operations Center 2, CIA Headquarters

Langley, Virginia

Leroux dropped into his seat, a smile on his face. Sherrie was deploying again today, so last night had been one hell of a ride, floors, tables, and counters buffed in all rooms of the apartment. He hadn't gotten any sleep in, but it was worth the sacrifice.

Randy Child, the team's tech wunderkind, entered the operations center and grinned at him. "Somebody got some last night."

Leroux gave him a look, his eyes darting over to Tong whose cheeks flushed as he caught her pained expression. She was still carrying a torch for him, and he hated to admit it, but there was a flicker of one on his end as well. He would never act on it, but it still racked him with guilt every time he found his mind drifting to some fantasy of what it would be like if they were together instead of him and Sherrie. "A gentleman never tells."

"That's a yes." Child dropped into his seat. "You're one lucky bastard, boss."

Leroux had to agree, but he did so silently. He *was* a lucky bastard. "Anything I need to know about?" he asked the room in general as he brought up the daily briefs.

Tong faced him. "The only thing out of the ordinary so far is the lack of response from the cartels."

"Still no activity?"

"Nothing. Quiet here and in Mexico."

Leroux frowned. "They're definitely up to something. There's no way in hell they'd do what they did then not follow it up when we didn't meet their demands."

"It's got to be the summit. It's too juicy a target."

Leroux agreed. "Everybody upstairs and at the Pentagon is with you, but Washington's determined to go ahead with the summit, and the Mexicans are assuring them they can provide security. Unfortunately, whoever's got the president's ear has convinced him that postponing, moving, or canceling the summit would be a sign of weakness."

Child spun in his chair, staring up at the ceiling. "He's right about that."

Tong eyed him. "You mean you think the president should go?"

Child dropped his foot, killing the spin. "Hell, no. I think he's an idiot for going. Sometimes a sign of weakness is a sign of wisdom. This isn't a penis-measuring contest with the cartels. This is life and death. If that summit goes ahead and the cartels are planning something, the president might survive, but how many security personnel are going to die trying to save him? It's arrogance at its worst, and a selfish act."

Leroux was impressed with the young man's assessment of the situation, an assessment he happened to agree with. "Look at you. Keep thinking like that and you might actually be running this place someday."

Child batted the idea away with a flick of his wrist. "Hell, no. I prefer to be behind the keyboard saving the day rather than in front of a bunch of suits taking credit."

"If that's what you think the chief does, then you don't know the man too well."

Child shrugged. "The chief's an enigma."

Leroux laughed. "Just remember, I used to be you. Someone smarter always comes along. You either mentor them, supervise them, or get the hell out of their way."

"So, is that why you're my supervisor?"

"I don't recall saying you were smarter than me."

Tong grinned. "I know I don't recall it."

Packman laughed. "Burned!"

Child flipped the man the bird and Leroux chuckled. "Sorry, Randy, but you walked into that one."

"Yeah, I suppose I did."

Leroux switched back to business. "How goes the hunt?"

He had tasked Child with identifying and locating the man who had apparently unified the cartels in the aftermath of the mass arrests. Identifying him had proven easier than expected. He had been wearing a hood that had openings for the eyes and mouth but nothing else, and his voice had been electronically altered, but a distinctive scar on his lower lip and the missing tip of his right index finger revealed as he stabbed it toward his audience gave him away.

It was Juan Garza, Salvador Garza's younger brother, a man with a reputation for being so vicious, the Mexican authorities and rival cartels didn't dare target the older brother for fear his sibling might take control.

It was yet another piece of intel that Washington had ignored. Salvador Garza should have been left alone. It forced Leroux to wonder when all was said and done, and the history of these events was written, would blame be placed where it should be, with the leaders who ultimately made the decisions, or with the minions like him who had provided the intel that was ignored? He suspected the latter should this new war on terror fail.

The smile on Child's face, however, gave him hope.

"You found something, didn't you?"

"Yep." Child tapped at his keyboard then gestured toward the main display. Two images appeared, one a frame grab from the message posted by Garza, the other an image of the older brother sitting behind an impressively ornate desk.

"What am I looking at?"

"I know where he recorded the message."

Leroux smiled. "Really?"

Child isolated a portion of each image, showing the wall above each man's right shoulder, a distinctive bookshelf revealed with an even more distinctive carving of a golden eagle featured prominently on the shelf.

Tong folded her arms as she leaned back. "That looks hand-carved, one of a kind."

Leroux agreed. "It's the same room." He turned to Child. "And we know where this photo of Salvador was taken?"

"In his private bunker. It's an underground facility that he claims is impervious to assault and that he can run the cartel from, for years if necessary."

Leroux grunted. "A few bunker-busters might have him thinking differently. Let's get some satellite coverage of this facility. See if we can confirm he's still there."

Child stared at anything but Leroux's face. "Well, that's going to be a problem."

Leroux regarded him. "What do you mean?"

"I mean, we know where this location is, but we don't really know *where* this location is."

"Huh?"

Tong stared at Child, exasperated. "What the hell are you talking about?"

Child jerked his chin toward the display. "The picture of Salvador Garza behind his desk was taken by a reporter two years ago who was brought to his secret compound for an interview. So, we know that it's his secret compound where the brother was when he recorded his message. The problem is that we don't know where that compound is, because the reporter was blindfolded, and the way she described it, she went through several vehicle transfers before she got there. She has no idea where the compound is actually located."

Leroux cursed. It was a dead end. Or was it? He wagged a finger. "Wait a minute. If this is the bunker that Salvador Garza claimed he could run his organization from, it's obviously extremely secure. If his brother was there a few days ago, then it makes sense that he's still there, using the location for its intended purpose. If they're planning something big, they have to know the hammer's going to come down on them, so they must be resupplying and bringing in their most senior people and closest family members. My guess is, some sort of alert went out ordering people to collection points. We need to identify anybody we think would be likely brought in, then try to trace them."

Tong worked her station and smiled. "I thought I remembered something." She pointed at the display, the image of a young man shown. "This is Raul Garza, Salvador and Juan's nephew. Rumor has it he's being groomed to replace Salvador should something happen, instead of Juan."

Child chewed his cheek. "But wouldn't that mean he'd want to leave him hanging out there to dry?"

"Or it could mean he wants to bring him in so he can't do any harm while Juan is holing up."

Leroux's head bobbed. "Keep your enemies close. It makes sense, but do we know where he is?"

Tong smiled. "He's at some car show in Monterey."

Leroux's eyebrows shot up. "California? Why haven't we picked him up?"

"Because he has no record. He's completely clean. The FBI's theory is that his uncle is keeping him squeaky clean while teaching him the business so that the authorities can't touch him. He can't be arrested for being a relative of a criminal, so he travels freely around the world. He's a huge car aficionado."

"When's he due to return to Mexico?"

"Today."

"How?"

Tong brought up a travel itinerary. "Would you believe he's flying commercial?"

Leroux smiled. "We need to get someone on that flight."

LAX

Los Angeles, California

Sherrie strode swiftly through LAX, just another frazzled passenger, the airline industry still a disaster post-pandemic. She had to wonder when the country would recover. It had lost nearly one in every 300 of its citizens in less than a year, far more than any other civilized country had. Plus, legal immigration had nearly ground to a halt during that time, leaving an even bigger deficit in the labor market. Not to mention a lot of people in high-risk professions opted for early retirement rather than put their lives at risk, and that included airline pilots and flight crews. It could take another decade for the country to recover, if not longer, with an entire generation seemingly content to live in Mom and Dad's house while they sought their bliss.

She couldn't imagine a life like that. She had to be doing something constructive, and serving in the way she did was not only her way of giving back to the country that had given her so much, but also of maintaining her sanity.

Idle hands are the Devil's playthings.

She needed outlets for her pent-up energy. When she was home, that was her boyfriend, and when she wasn't, it was the job. And today, she had a chance to seek revenge for the thousands that were dead after the Night of Reckoning. She had been tasked to track Raul Garza, Salvador Garza's nephew.

Raul was boarding a plane to Los Mochis, a plane that Langley had already delayed along with several dozen other flights to allay suspicions Raul's was being targeted. The moment she was at the gate, the flight would begin boarding, but that all depended on Raul actually showing up.

"Any sign of him?" she asked, momentarily covering her mouth.

Leroux replied over the earpiece tucked deep in her ear canal. "Recommend radio silence. He's twenty feet in front of you. Pink shirt."

She spotted him just ahead, lined up at security, and her heart rate picked up slightly. The mission was on, and should she succeed, America might just deliver justice for the thousands of innocents that had paid the ultimate price.

Fort Cavazos

Outside Killeen, Texas

Dawson stretched, wincing slightly, though not as much as yesterday and even less so than the day before.

"How are you feeling?" asked Red.

"Pretty good. A little stiff, but I can work those kinks out. I'm guessing I'll be cleared for active duty when I see the doc later."

"Good. I just received our orders from HQ." Red wagged a tablet. "We're being deployed to Mexico City as part of a rapid reaction force should something go wrong."

Dawson shook his head. "So, the Secret Service is still insisting on providing all American security?"

"Yep, though I don't think the blame really lies with them. The Mexicans apparently are saying they don't want any American military involved in the security since they're blaming us for the current situation."

Dawson grunted as he continued to stretch. "You can't blame them for that, I suppose."

"No. The president stepped in, however, and insisted on the rapid reaction force."

"What's it consist of?"

"Four Delta and two Canadian JTF 2 teams."

Dawson's eyebrows rose. "No Mexicans?"

"No. The Mexicans said they didn't want any part of it because they didn't want to condone foreign forces on their soil. The Canadian prime minister offered two of their teams to balance things out a bit, and the Mexican president agreed."

Dawson bent over, touching his toes. "Good. I'd rather have Canadian teams than Mexican any day. The cartels' infiltration inside the Mexican army and law enforcement is way too deep. And as we both know, those crazy Canucks are awesome in a firefight. I'd let them watch my back any day."

"Me too."

"When do we deploy?"

"Tonight. There's a staging area at the naval air base outside Mexico City where the Mexicans will be hosting us."

"What are they letting us go in with?"

"Blackhawks and Apaches, plus any weapons and ammo we can carry. I didn't mention that Atlas can carry a tank."

Dawson grinned at his friend. "I like how you think. Make sure we have some heavy weapons in the mix, including Stingers. I've got a bad feeling about this."

"You're not the only one. Unfortunately, they're refusing to let us bring anything that explodes."

Dawson rolled his eyes. "Fine. There's nothing we can do about that now." He shook out his body, relaxing every muscle. "All right. Time to see the doctor and get that medical clearance. Make sure the boys are ready for tonight. I've got a really bad feeling about this."

Los Mochis International Airport

Los Mochis, Mexico

Sherrie climbed in the passenger seat of the beat-up pale-gray sedan and closed the door, the friendly greeting she had exchanged with the driver when she first arrived at the airport hopefully giving anyone who might have been watching, the impression they were old friends. Oscar Rivas pulled them away from the curb and into traffic, his phone mounted to the dash indicating they were two kilometers away from their target. An asset at LAX had tagged Raul Garza's luggage, and Langley had confirmed through their camera taps in Los Mochis that Raul's people had collected the luggage and loaded it into the SUV sent to pick him up.

Sherrie frowned as the car backfired. "Are you sure this thing is reliable?"

Rivas gave her a look, throwing a hand toward the hood. "Do you see a leaping jungle cat sitting out there? Of course she's reliable." He patted the dash, cooing. "You don't listen to her, girl, I know you'll never let me down."

Sherrie chuckled then pulled out her laptop and opened it. She logged in then brought up the live satellite feed. She pointed. "There they are. SUV with two escorts front and back. A little conspicuous."

Rivas disagreed. "Not really in Mexico these days. Anybody with money travels with heavy security, and this guy's got a clean record. Even if the police had the balls to pull him over, it wouldn't be for anything more than a traffic stop. The locals and the Federales have probably been informed of his arrival by his own people, just to make sure there's no foolishness. All we need to do is make sure we don't lose him and don't get spotted. What do you think the chances are he's going to lead us straight to the compound?"

"I can't see it. They've managed to keep it secret so far. Nobody has a clue where it is. They're not going to go easy on security now. We're probably going to have to go through several exchanges. Are you prepared for that?"

Rivas nodded. "I've got my own personal contacts that I can call to do our own exchanges. The cartels have been known to use drones, so I wouldn't be surprised if they've got one parked over their guy right now, watching for anything following him."

"You're probably right."

"What's the plan if we do find this compound?"

Sherrie shook her head. "Above my pay grade. But if it were up to me, I'd pound it into dust."

Fort Cavazos

Outside Killeen, Texas

Dawson boarded the chopper, the last boot of the team to leave the ground. They lifted off a moment later, several dozen transport and escort airframes joining them. He took a seat beside Red then leaned back, resting his head against the vibrating hold. He always found it relaxing, like a vibrating massage chair. He glanced over at his best friend, uncharacteristically quiet. "Any word?"

"No. The doctor said he'd have the results tomorrow."

"You should be with her. It's not too late."

Red jerked his thumb at the window behind him. "I kind of think it is."

Dawson flashed him a grin. "We're not too high. I can kick you out."

Red chuckled. "While I'd love to be there, Shirley is insisting we treat this as nothing until it isn't. If I'm there while you guys are out on an op as critical as this, that means I think her situation is more important, which means it's cancer."

Dawson's head bobbed. He could understand the thinking. Right now, Red's wife had a lump that had been biopsied, and most times with women her age, it was nothing, so there was no point in panicking. Not yet. "Smart thinking."

"We're going to treat it as nothing until it isn't."

Niner chimed in, and Dawson prepared for something inappropriate. "You know, I think this is a valuable lesson for all of us."

Spock cocked an eyebrow. "How so?"

"Well, I know after I heard about Shirley's situation, I gave Angela a thorough examination when we got home." He grinned. "Three times."

Atlas leaned forward, holding up four fingers. "I did the same with Vanessa."

Niner gave him the eye. "Four times? Bullshit. If I had said five, would you have held up six fingers?"

"But you didn't, did you?"

Niner turned to Dawson. "So, how about you?"

Atlas' eyebrows shot up at the audacity of asking the team lead such a question.

Dawson regarded Niner. "A real man knows how to get the job done the first time."

The team roared with laughter at Niner's expense and the little man simply shrugged, jerking a thumb at the massive Atlas. "Hey, it took him four tries."

Atlas punched Niner on the shoulder, sending him reeling into Jimmy. "Don't make me explain the concept of encores to you."

Spock's eyebrows shot up. "Isn't that where the audience isn't satisfied with the length of the show, so they demand the band play more?"

Niner extended a fist and Spock bumped. "Good one."

Dawson held up a hand. "Okay, that's enough. Last thing we need is Atlas whipping out his anaconda to disprove Spock's theory."

Atlas jabbed a finger at the widower warrior. "I guarantee you don't want that, little man."

Niner leaned up close to Atlas. "It is a sight to behold."

Atlas shoved him away. "I agree. And I've told you to stop looking." He became serious. "What do you think we're facing?"

Dawson wagged his tablet. "If the last intel is correct, either nothing or a world of hurt."

"What do you mean?" asked Jimmy.

"The cartels are quiet. Even their regular bullshit has stopped. Local police that aren't on the take have reported that they think a lot of the cartels' foot soldiers have left their local areas. Langley thinks they're heading to Mexico City, though the Federales are denying that, saying there's no evidence to back that up. They've also implemented a security cordon around the city with random searches. They're claiming they've found nothing."

Niner leaned back, folding his arms. "There's no damn way the cartels are going to give up a juicy target like this. If I were them, the moment I heard the summit was going through, I would have moved every weapon I could into that city, then sent my people in after them unarmed."

Dawson agreed. "That's one of the scenarios Langley's suggested. If there's nothing going on, then we've got nothing to worry about. We'll just hole up at the base, then when the president leaves, return home. So that's a scenario we don't even need to plan for. The question is, if they are up to something, what is it? Is it just a disruption, a show of force where they perform a bunch of random attacks around the city that forces the foreign leaders to evacuate therefore embarrassing the Mexican government? Or are they planning something more serious, like an assassination attempt on our president in retaliation for what he ordered?"

"I'd be leaning to option A," said Red. "It's the least risky for them and certainly achievable. Two or three mass casualty events around the city and the Secret Service will be pulling the president out within minutes. It demonstrates the cartels' power, embarrasses the Mexican president, then they threaten another Night of Reckoning back home while reiterating their demands."

"Definitely plausible," agreed Dawson. "And if that's the case, we might not even be deployed. Or if we are, we won't reach the president before his motorcade arrives at the airport."

"We should be with him," said Atlas.

"You won't get any argument from me, but the Mexicans said no military. If the shit hits the fan, we'll be sitting in these choppers and we're ten minutes out. If the evac goes smoothly, he'll be on Air Force One before we get there. If it doesn't, then hopefully we'll be there in time to make a difference and extract him ourselves."

Red frowned. "Let's hope it doesn't get to that. But I've got a bad feeling about this, now that I think about it. If I were the cartels, I'd be pouring everybody I had into that city to cause complete and utter chaos. And let's not forget the fact that they've got Stingers. We saw them at the raid the other night. They have enough personnel and heavy weaponry that they could block any escape route they have planned for the president, and because of those Stingers, taking him out by air isn't really an option."

Niner raised a finger. "Um, aren't we going in by chopper?"

"Yep."

Niner pursed his lips. "Shouldn't we at least discuss that?"

"Nope. No choice. If we go in by ground, we'll just be caught up in traffic or whatever chaos the cartels have managed to create. No, gentlemen, we are going in like airborne cavalry. Let's just pray God's on our side."

National Palace

Mexico City, Mexico

"Sir, do you have a minute?"

Director General Fernando Trujilo glanced up from his laptop then gestured for his aide, Luis Arias, to enter. "Only a minute. I'm briefing the president in five. What have you got for me?"

Arias held up a tablet. "It's not good, sir. We received a report from perimeter security of a carload of four men with gang tattoos trying to enter the city."

Trujilo paused. "Was there an incident?"

"They were unarmed. The vehicle was searched and no weapons were found, but one of the officers gained access to one of their cellphones and found an image showing the route the American president will be taking from the airport to the palace."

Trujilo tensed. "Did he say how he got it?"

"No. As soon as it was discovered, they ran and our men shot them."

"They're dead?"

"Yes, sir. All four of them."

Trujilo cursed. "We can't question the dead."

"Sir, how would they have gotten the route? We've set up security on three different possible routes. There's no way they could know which of them was the real one. Not unless they had someone on the inside."

Trujilo had to agree. There was a leak somewhere. "Fine. There's nothing we can do about it now. When the president arrives tomorrow, I'll inform his security detail that we're changing to one of the alternate routes."

"Which one?"

"I'll decide that, and I won't be telling anyone until we actually make the switch. That way, we don't have to worry about leaks."

"Good thinking, sir. Oh, you should know that after I received this report, I issued orders that all males with gang tattoos should be turned away and refused entry to the city, and any found on the street are to be arrested and detained."

Trujilo pursed his lips, pissed that his subordinate had overstepped his authority. He drew a calming breath. "That was the right call. But next time, you clear it with me first."

Arias' eyes bulged. "Yes, sir. Sorry, sir. I just knew how busy you were and felt it was what you would have done."

"It was. If you haven't already, officially issue the orders citywide in my name, then have them report back on how many they're turning away and how many they're detaining. I want to try to get a sense of how big a problem we may be dealing with."

"Yes, sir. Right away, sir."

"Does anyone else know about the map?"

"No, sir. I don't think the officers recognized the significance."

"Keep it that way." Trujilo flicked his fingers toward the door. "Now get out of here. I have to meet the president."

Arias bowed slightly then disappeared as Trujilo snapped his laptop shut and rose, his underling's report having him gravely concerned. Now the question was, what to do about it?

Outside El Carrizo, Mexico

Sherrie dropped into the passenger seat and closed the door, immediately flipping open her laptop as Rivas exchanged pleasantries with the man who had brought them their new car. Raul Garza had switched cars twenty minutes ago and Langley had isolated the footage to show that he and his entourage had been blindfolded when they got out of their original vehicle. It appeared the man's uncle was keeping the location of their bunker secret even from the closest of allies.

Rivas climbed in and started the engine, sweet air conditioning blowing from the vents. It was a smoking hot day, as she supposed every day was in Mexico, but she lived in Virginia where they had winters, and was often on ops in Russia where they definitely had winters. She was not a fan of the heat. Sunbathing on the rooftop of their apartment building was one thing. That was voluntary. To live in this heat day in and day out was something she simply couldn't imagine, though she assumed one would get used to it after a while.

Rivas stuck the GPS tracker to the dash, Langley confirming the luggage from the airport had been transferred, the cartels so far not suspecting anything untoward was going on.

She glanced over her shoulder as Rivas' contact drove away in their original beater. "Do you trust him?"

"With my life. He's my brother-in-law."

Sherrie smirked. "I hope you get along with your sister."

He laughed. "I'd be more concerned with whether *he* gets along with my sister."

Sherrie gestured at the map. "Any idea where they're heading?"

He reached forward, pinching his fingers on the display, zooming the map out, then pointed. "It's obviously the Sierra Madre Occidental range. I'm guessing somewhere near Copper Canyon."

"The only description we have from that reporter's interview is him saying it's built into the side of a mountain, so it makes sense."

"And if it's true, that could be a problem."

"How?"

"If this place is in the mountains, then you know the roads in and out are going to be few in number and closely watched. There's no way we're going to be able to approach."

"You're probably right, which is why we'll leave it to the drones and the satellites if we get to that point. For our next exchange, make sure your cousin or nephew or whomever you're going to have meeting us brings hiking and camping equipment and some weapons, just in case."

"My uncle is already on it."

Sherrie regarded him. "Just how big is your family?"

"Big."

"Big enough?"

"Absolutely. And don't worry, we actually all like each other."

Base Aeronaval de Mexico

Mexico City, Mexico

Dawson lay in his rack, his eyes closed, his hands clasped on his chest as he relaxed, listening to the camaraderie of the four different Delta teams and the two Canadian Joint Task Force 2 teams. They were all brothers in arms, allies in whatever fight they happened to be involved in on any given day.

Niner approached. "BD, you've gotta try one of these things, they're incredible."

Dawson opened his eyes to see Niner standing at the foot of his bunk holding something in his hands. "What the hell is that?"

"The Canadians call it a BeaverTail."

Dawson cocked an eyebrow. "That sounds disgusting."

"That's what I said. But remember when we met up with those guys in Syria, they said they'd bring us some, and they did."

Red held his own up from the far end of the room. "Trust me, BD, try it."

Dawson sat up and took the rectangular box in Niner's hand, finding a pastry inside that was long and flat. "A beaver tail, huh?"

The JTF 2 team lead, Master Warrant Officer Cyril Dwyer, strolled over. "It's 'BeaverTail, *eh*.' You're talking about a Canadian concoction there."

Dawson laughed. "Okay, eh, I'll try it." He took a bite, an explosion of cinnamon, sugar, and lemon filling his mouth. He chewed, his eyes shooting wide as a smile spread. "Holy shit! You weren't kidding. And you Canadians eat these things?"

"Well, not daily."

Dawson laughed, taking another bite, beckoning Atlas over. "See if you can save one of these for Vanessa."

"Why, you think she'd like it?"

"To hell with that. I want her to recreate it. I don't want to have to fly to Canada every time I want one of these."

Atlas gave a thumbs-up. "Good thinking. We'll steal their idea and make it more American."

Dwyer regarded him. "How the hell would you make it more American?"

Niner held his up. "A bourbon dipping sauce."

Red grinned. "Yeah. Replace the lemon with a drizzle of Kentucky's finest."

Dwyer dismissed the idea. "Doesn't work. I already tried it with rye. Trust me, this concoction is perfect the way it is, and there are other flavors, none of which involve alcohol."

Niner chuckled. "Don't you worry, we'll figure out a way."

"Well, when you do, you let me know." Dwyer became serious. "So, BD, what do you think we're getting into?"

Dawson stood, continuing to work on his pastry. "Nothing good if that last flash I just read is any indication."

Dwyer agreed. "The good thing is someone finally thought to close off the city to obvious hostiles, but my guess is it's too little, too late. Not to mention the fact that all they've done is block off the roadways. These guys can walk in on foot if they want to. It's not like there's a wall around the city with only a few access points."

"They should be calling this thing off," said Niner as he licked his fingers. "This is too damn dangerous for a political statement."

Dawson shook his head. "I can't see them doing that. This thing is going ahead unless something major happens before the president gets on the ground. Let's just make sure we're all prepared for a worst-case scenario. I have a bad feeling that the Night of Reckoning was just a warm-up act."

Garza Cartel Compound

Somewhere in the Sierra Madre Occidental Mountains, Mexico

Garza smashed his fist on the desk as he cursed, the contents rattling as he processed the report from Mexico City. The police were turning away their men en masse. Perhaps having foot soldiers prove their loyalty by how many square feet of ink they sported wasn't the wisest of things. "How does this affect our plans?"

His contact in Mexico City shook his head. "Not significantly. Most of the guys you're sending here don't have any visible tattoos, and some of them have none at all. Besides, my last update indicates you have over two thousand people already inside the city limits. More than enough to do the job. The important thing is that we got the weapons in ahead of time."

"Including the Stingers?"

"Oh, yeah. If they decide to evacuate the president by helicopter, he doesn't stand a chance. But I doubt they'll be that stupid. My counterpart has indicated none of the extraction plans include helicopters. They know about your Stingers."

"Any indication they're changing the route?"

"No."

"Good, then our plans don't change. Tomorrow, America pays for what it's done to my family."

Arias Residence

Mexico City, Mexico

Arias sighed, his shoulders slumping as he turned off the engine, his eyes burning with fatigue, working as Director General Trujilo's aide exhausting. This was the first time he had been home in two days, and he couldn't wait to hold his wife in his arms and tuck in his children, who should already be asleep at this hour. Tomorrow, in fact, the next three days of the summit, would be even busier, and he couldn't wait for this to be over. It was foolish having this event. Everyone in private agreed, but the president had already lost face by granting the Americans permission to operate militarily on Mexican soil, and he wasn't about to lose further face by showing any fear of the cartels.

It made for long, difficult days, but it would soon be over, then it would be three years before Mexico hosted the summit again, unless another American president decided his country's two closest neighbors weren't worth his time.

He stepped out of his car and locked the doors before checking the gate to make certain it was secure. He wasn't overly concerned. A police unit was stationed outside, all senior government officials given additional security since the Americans' fiasco. He entered his home of ten years, the only home his children had ever known, and gently closed the door, not wanting to wake anyone, though he was certain his wife would be on the couch waiting for him, having fallen asleep watching her shows. He kicked off his shoes and loosened his tie, smiling at the television playing in the living room.

"Hey, my love, are you awake?" he asked as he entered the room. There was no response and he rounded the couch, smiling at the sight of her feet, the love of his life, the only woman he had ever loved, curled up on the couch, sound asleep as he had suspected. He gently moved the blanket from his wife's face, the covering hand-crocheted by her grandmother, a wedding gift to them both.

And cried out at the bullet hole in the center of her forehead, blood trickling down on the couch, her face pale.

A sound behind him had him spinning. Two men stood near the kitchen, both with handguns pointed at him, silencers in place. He raised his hands, tears already flowing at what had happened to his wife. "Please, I don't care what you do to me, but leave my children alone."

One of the men stepped forward, raising his weapon and pointing it directly at Arias' chest. "I'm afraid it's too late for that. You interfered in our business, and that can't be allowed."

The man squeezed the trigger twice and Arias' body jerked with each hit, though curiously, it didn't hurt, at least not initially. Then he gasped as he collapsed to his knees, a searing pain in his chest overwhelming him, and he stared down to see his crisp white shirt rapidly turning crimson as his failing heart pumped his blood onto the expensive linen. He fell to his side and reached up with his last ounce of strength, placing his hand on his wife's cold cheek.

I'll be with you soon, my love.

Aeropuerto Internacional Benito Juarez

Mexico City, Mexico

Florencia Torres descended the steps of Air Force One, her heart racing with excitement. This was the first time she had been in Mexico, the country of her parents. Born in San Diego, she considered herself as American as anyone. She had attended public school, worked her ass off, got the grades and got the scholarship, went to a good college, then managed to get a job at the White House, working only yards away from the big man himself.

It was a thrilling job, even when it was boring. She was a social media coordinator and went on a lot of these trips, taking photos and drafting posts for the various feeds the White House controlled. She didn't have the power yet to post, but perhaps in a year or two she might be trusted enough should her drafts continue to be approved as is.

Unfortunately, she had no time to enjoy herself and take in the sights. Using her phone, she snapped a shot of the president's car, nicknamed The Beast, as it pulled away with its Mexican police escort, along with a couple of dozen Secret Service vehicles. She climbed into the back of an SUV assigned to her and scurried over to the far side as two more of her coworkers joined her.

The door slammed shut and the driver pulled away, glancing in his rearview mirror. "You don't get out unless I say so, and you don't put the windows down. And put your seatbelts on, this could be a bit of a bumpy ride. The roads aren't good, and we'll be moving at a decent clip."

As if to prove his point, he took a left-hand turn hard, sending everyone sliding to the passenger side. She scrambled back into position and grabbed her seatbelt, jerking it over her torso and clicking it in place.

The driver grinned. "Told you. Even the president's wearing his seatbelt today."

"I hope so."

They had been given a detailed security briefing before they left, the most intense she had ever received. It was clear the Secret Service was concerned that the cartels would try something. Every country she had visited so far on the job had been civilized, friendly, and secure. This was the first time she had been somewhere that wasn't safe, but that just added to the excitement. She would be fine. Nobody was better at this than the Secret Service, and apparently there were Special Forces on standby not far from here that could reach them within ten minutes should something go wrong.

Their vehicle was bulletproof, and holding out for ten minutes should be easy, especially with all the police and military lining the route. She peered out the tinted windows at the crowds lining the roadway, held back by concrete barriers bolted into the ground and a cordon of heavily armed police. A lump formed in her throat.

It was intimidating.

"You okay?"

She turned to Carl Anderson, sitting beside her, and forced a brave face. "Yeah, just excited."

"That's good," said the man only two years older than her but with a wealth of international travel experience. "We'll be fine, but if something does happen, just listen to the Secret Service."

"Or the police."

He dismissed her suggestion. "No. Only listen to our guys. Whatever you do, don't trust the police. Too many of them here are bought and paid for."

Sweat trickled down her back despite the generous amount of air conditioning blowing through the cabin. If they couldn't trust those meant to protect them, then what the hell were they doing here? When she had told her father where she was going, he was pissed. The Night of Reckoning had woken up America to just how vulnerable it was. Thousands were dead, but fortunately, as far as she was aware, her family had escaped the carnage. Yet friends of hers hadn't. All throughout America, families were grieving, friends were mourning, and neighbors were thankful they had been spared.

Her father hadn't wanted her to go and advised her to quit her job if they made her, but there was no way she would do that. This was part of the job, and if she wanted to make a career of it, quitting out of cowardice on her first challenging assignment would swiftly put an end to it. She stared out the window at the police, their faces all covered by masks so the cartels couldn't identify them, and it had her wondering how could the Mexicans even know who was behind the masks, and whether they could be trusted?

She shivered.

Maybe Dad was right.

Garza Cartel Compound

Somewhere in the Sierra Madre Occidental Mountains, Mexico

"The job's been done and there's no indication word has spread. You're sure you still don't want us to hit him on the way in?"

Garza shook his head. "No. We can't be certain that one of the police officers involved didn't inform his superiors. We'll go with Plan B. It was always the better one anyway."

"I think that's the right call, sir. So, we begin as previously discussed?"

"Yes, five minutes into the broadcast, signal our men to begin. I want Mexico City paralyzed."

"Don't worry, sir, we'll put on one hell of a show."

"See that you do." Garza ended the call then leaned back in his chair, closing his eyes. His chair. It was actually his brother's, but the longer he sat here running things, the more he wanted it. Deep down, he had always wanted it. He had enjoyed being an enforcer for years. He loved pulling the trigger, stabbing the knife, delivering the jaw-shattering punch. If his knuckles throbbed from a good beating at the end of the day, then it was a good day.

But the boss never got his hands dirty, and perhaps that was a good thing. If he were to become boss, should something happen to his brother, he would miss the fun. But the power this position held was exhilarating. He could order anyone in the world dead. It didn't matter who. Most people didn't understand the power the cartels wielded. Most thought of them simply as gangs. They couldn't fathom the amount of money involved. If they were listed on the stock exchange, they would rank among the most valuable companies in the world, and with that kind of money came unbelievable power. It was simply that the cartels chose not to exercise it. If they wanted a president dead, he would be dead. If they wanted a prime minister dead, he would be dead. It didn't matter. But doing so would bring undue attention, and that was bad for business.

Kill rival gang members and the dregs of society, nobody cared—most simply shrugged and said they deserved it. The Night of Reckoning, as the Americans were calling it, was a demonstration of their power, of what the cartels could truly do should America pursue its war. This wasn't like 9/11 where so much had to go right in order for the attack to succeed. This was something they could repeat night after night if they wanted to. And what they had accomplished had been barely planned.

Now they were coordinating the next attack should their demands not be met. If today didn't go as planned, the next retaliation would leave the thin blue line that protected America dripping with blood.

National Palace

Mexico City, Mexico

Florencia snapped another photo of the three foreign leaders shaking hands as scores of cameras flashed, the press corps in a frenzy. They had arrived unscathed, and she felt completely safe now that she was within the National Palace grounds. The next excitement would be at the end of the day when they moved to the hotel, but staffers like her wouldn't be part of that motorcade.

And that was this evening's problem. For now, all she cared about was doing her job and doing it well, while enjoying the excitement of it all.

She noticed a vibration in her feet and she looked down at the marble floor. It stopped and she shrugged, raising her phone once again to take another photo. There was second vibration and this time others noticed it as well, a hush falling over the room as most of the cameras fell silent.

The floor vibrated again, but this time it was accompanied by a rumble in the distance. Somebody screamed and everyone turned to see a woman pointing out a window, a fireball on the horizon.

And a flurry of coordinated panic kicked in.

The Secret Service burst into action, rushing the stage, grabbing a confused president by both arms, half-dragging, half-carrying him from the room as Canadian and Mexican security teams did the same with their leaders. Anderson grabbed her by the arm, hauling her toward the exit they had been briefed on to use should there be an emergency evacuation. More explosions shook the room and gunfire rattled in the distance. Her heart hammered and her pulse pounded in her ears as her vision clouded, her eyes mere pinpoints as she lost focus.

"Breathe!"

She flinched at Anderson's voice and sucked in a breath, not realizing she had been holding it.

"Keep breathing or you're going to pass out."

She inhaled again, the world around her snapping back into focus, and she found herself in a rear corridor, panicked staffers from three nations rushing toward their evac points. Armed security lined the walls, ushering them along, funneling everyone toward a rear courtyard. Helicopters thundering overhead had her thanking God her president had escaped.

More explosions shook the ground.

"How many is that?" asked someone.

Anderson replied. "Eight, I think."

"Holy shit! They're going to lay waste to the city!" cried someone else.

"Then we'd better get the hell out of here before they do."

Gunfire directly ahead had the entire procession skidding to a halt, everyone ducking. These shots weren't from the streets, these were inside the palace grounds.

The fight had already reached them.

Base Aeronaval de Mexico

Mexico City, Mexico

Dawson cursed as he spotted the first fireball erupt from the city on the horizon. He reached forward and slapped the pilot of the idling Black Hawk on the shoulder. "Let's go! Let's go! Let's go!"

"I don't have orders."

"Screw orders!" Dawson pointed toward the city as a second explosion sounded. "The attack's begun. Seconds count."

The pilot cursed, powering up the machine as he activated his comms, the whines of the other choppers around them growing in pitch as the rapid reaction force of American and Canadian Special Forces sprang into action without waiting for orders that would merely delay the response.

They lifted off the ground as Dawson activated his comms. "Control, Bravo Zero-One. Sit rep, over."

Clancy responded a moment later. "Zero-One, Control Actual. We have reports of multiple explosions throughout Mexico City. Stand by for permission to deploy from the Mexican authorities, over."

"Copy that, Control. Be advised, I've already given the order to deploy, over."

He could almost hear Clancy smiling. "I would expect nothing less, Zero-One. Proceed toward the palace. We're trying to get an exact fix on the president's situation."

"Copy that, Control."

"ETA eight minutes!" shouted the pilot.

"Control, our ETA is eight minutes, over."

"Copy that, Zero-One. Let's hope it's not all over before you get there."

National Palace

Mexico City, Mexico

The gunfire on the other side of the door abruptly fell silent, the throng of staffers cowering on the floor slowly rising. The doors burst open and a Mexican guard beckoned them. "It's clear! Let's go! Let's go!"

Another explosion ripped through the city, a wave of startled yelps and cries the response.

"We have to go now!" he shouted. "The convoy is leaving with or without you!"

Anderson grabbed Florencia's arm, hauling her to her feet. "Let's go, everyone!" he shouted. Those gathered slowly rose, most still crouching, though the evacuation picked up speed as the guns remained silent in the rear courtyard.

She followed Anderson through the doors and into the bright afternoon light. Scores of vehicles were waiting and she searched for her driver when one of the Secret Service agents beckoned the front of the group.

"Take any one! It doesn't matter! We're all heading to the same place! Canadians and Americans, let's go! Let's go!"

The crowd surged forward and she rushed toward the nearest SUV. She stumbled, but Anderson's grip on her arm tightened and he hauled her back upright.

"Are you okay?"

She nodded, but she wasn't. She was terrified. Tears were streaming down her face, her breathing was rapid, and it was a constant struggle simply to maintain consciousness. She so wanted to pass out. She so wanted to be back home.

She so wanted to be in her daddy's arms.

They reached an open rear door and she dove inside, Anderson following, three more joining them in the rear. The back row filled up then someone leaped into the passenger seat, smacking a hand on the dash. "Let's get the hell out of here!"

The Secret Service agent behind the wheel put the car in gear and pulled away, joining a line of other hastily overloaded vehicles as they slowly rolled through the gates. Anderson leaned forward, pointing ahead at three helicopters. "Is that the president?"

Before he got an answer, something streaked across the sky and Florencia gasped as whatever it was slammed into one of the helicopters, a small fireball erupting as the massive piece of machinery fell to the ground. Small explosions emerged from the other two and her eyes bulged. "What's happening?"

"Chaff," reported one of the Secret Service agents from the front. "Here they come!" More missiles streaked across the city, the decoys fooling several of them but not all of them. A second missile blasted into one of the choppers, then a third found the final one, and Florencia buried her face in her hands, unable to witness the horror.

"Oh my God! They killed the president!"

En route to Presidential Motorcade

Mexico City, Mexico

Dawson frowned as the third airframe fall from the sky, three good crews possibly dead, willingly sacrificing themselves to save their president. He just prayed it wasn't a futile effort, and that the crews had actually survived. They were low enough to the ground that they could survive the impact. It would be whether they were caught in secondary explosions or ambushed on the ground by a city overrun by the cartels.

"We're sure the president wasn't on board?" asked Niner.

"Unless they changed the plan, the helos were decoys. He should be in The Beast as part of a convoy heading to the airport."

Clancy's voice came in over Dawson's earpiece. "This is Control Actual. Sierra and Tango Teams, break off and secure the crash sites. Tend to the wounded, recover any bodies, destroy the equipment, and prepare for evac. Until rescue teams arrive on the ground, shoot anything with a gun. Don't trust the locals. We have multiple reports of hostiles in police and army uniforms. Your rules of engagement permit you to do whatever is necessary to protect the lives of American and Canadian citizens. All other teams, continue toward the National Palace. We'll update you en route as to where the convoy is. Control, out."

Dawson watched as the two Canadian choppers banked away, changing their heading slightly, now racing across the rooftops toward the smoldering wreckage on the horizon.

Niner sat back. "I kinda wish we were going with them."

"Me too," agreed Atlas. "Those poor bastards never stood a chance. They're the heroes, not a president who ignored advice."

While Dawson agreed with the sentiment, it was chatter that could be picked up by an open comm. "Stow the chit-chat, gentlemen, and remember the mission. Our job is to protect the president, and the flight crews had the same mission. We've all been in choppers that have been shot down before. As long as you're not too high up and survive the initial impact, you're usually good. The Canadians will secure them and get them out of there. Our job is the president, no matter who we think is to blame for this situation."

"Yes, Sergeant Major," echoed Niner and Atlas.

"Attention, this is Control Actual." Dawson held up a finger, silencing everyone. "The president's motorcade has come under coordinated attack less than two klicks from the National Palace. You'll be inserting into a hot LZ. Team leads on the ground have operational discretion. Do whatever it takes. Airstrikes have been authorized and will be executed as directed from the ground. Let's try to minimize civilian casualties. However, the security of the president and the Canadian prime minister are paramount, over."

Dawson activated his comms. "Control, Bravo Zero-One, what's the twenty on the Canadian prime minister?"

"He's in The Beast with the president," replied Clancy.

Spock cocked an eyebrow. "Interesting. I wonder if that was part of the plan."

Dawson shook his head. "No plan I read."

"Copy that, Control. As per the briefing, I'm taking over as senior." He was already staring at his tablet, a live satellite feed showing the motorcade trapped, some sort of barricade erected in front of it, gunfire from over a dozen positions raining down on the helpless occupants. "Instruct Secret Service to remain inside their vehicles. Order strafing runs from the Apaches from north to south on either side of the motorcade. Let's see if we can silence some of the small arms fire, over."

"Copy that, Zero-One. Control Actual to all teams, Bravo Zero-One now has operational control on the ground. Control retains ultimate authority. Acknowledge."

A string of acknowledgments from the other teams came through the comms.

"ETA to that motorcade?" asked Dawson.

"Four minutes!" replied the pilot. "I can shave maybe a minute off that, but it makes us more vulnerable to those Stingers."

"Negative. Continue evasive maneuvers. We're no good to the president if we're dead."

Two Apache gunships raced past them, speeding toward the area to execute his orders. Dawson turned to his team, all checking their equipment. "We're gonna insert hot and hard. Get on the ground, find cover, and shoot anything that's shooting in the direction of the convoy or yourself. Atlas, Niner, you're in charge of clearing whatever the hell is blocking the road. I wanna have this motorcade underway in less than five minutes of our arrival."

"What if we can't clear it?" asked Atlas.

"Then we either find another route to the airport or we fall back to the palace. I have no intention of letting the president die in Mexico City. Not on my watch."

Presidential Motorcade

Mexico City, Mexico

"What do we do?" screamed someone from the back row as Florencia huddled behind the driver's seat, Anderson's body draped over her as gunshots rang out around them, some pinging off the reinforced skin of their SUV.

"We need to get out of here!" yelled someone, their voice in a panic.

The Secret Service agent in the passenger seat put the kibosh on that idea. "The safest place for us now is inside this car. If you step outside, you'll be killed. We just need to hold out until relief arrives."

"What relief?" cried Florencia. "Who the hell is gonna save us from this shit?"

"We have Special Forces teams less than four minutes out and air support arriving any second now. Just keep your heads down and keep calm and follow my orders. You *will* survive this."

"Here they come!" announced the driver. "Everybody, stay as low as you can."

"What's happening?" she asked, squeezing her eyes shut.

"Help has arrived."

The loudest gun she had ever heard opened up from behind them, destruction raining down on the street just on the other side of the door she was pressed against. The noise was overwhelming, and rapidly passed their position, continuing down the road, the thunder of a helicopter overhead following it.

Anderson lifted off her, no doubt to take a look. "Holy shit!"

And she couldn't resist. She pulled herself up by her fingers and peered out. The street and sidewalks were torn apart, bodies strewn about. The gunfire resumed, though much of it now appeared directed at the sky.

"Here they come again!" warned the driver. She peered forward and he spotted her in the rearview mirror. "Get the hell down!"

Her heart slammed with the shame of being caught and she dropped back to the floor, Anderson pressing down on her once again as death from above punished their enemy, hopefully buying them the time they needed before the Special Forces teams arrived to rescue them. The only question was, how the hell could they possibly save so many if helicopters could be shot out of the sky and the roads blocked with impunity?

We're all gonna die.

Belme Residence, West Luzon Drive

Fort Liberty, North Carolina

"Maggie, you have to see this!"

Maggie rushed down the hallway, joining the others in the Belme's living room. Everyone huddled around the television as the children played in the backyard, blissfully unaware of what was going on with their fathers. She sat beside Shirley who grabbed her hand, squeezing it hard as Maggie took stock of what was playing out on the screen. It was a live report from a CNN reporter embedded with the motorcade. The cameraman and the reporter were inside the back of what appeared to be an SUV, the camera pressed against the window revealing the chaos outside, the gunfire non-stop.

"*—continue to be under heavy fire. The president's motorcade hasn't moved in more than five minutes, and the Mexican authorities seem powerless. It's clear that the cartels now control Mexico City, and as you saw from earlier footage where gunfire was being exchanged between police and military units, the loyalty of those assigned to protect the foreign guests is now in question. Two gunships just strafed the area several* *times. From our vantage point, it was impossible to see any markings, but we have to assume that since the convoy wasn't hit, we weren't their target. Our Secret Service escort assured us help is on the way, however, I can't give you any details as to when they might arrive. As we know, the cartels will be monitoring—"*

"Then get the hell off the air, you dumb bitch!" cried Vanessa.

"I realize you can't give specifics, Aynslee, but were you given any indication of whether it's minutes from now, half an hour from now, an hour? And in what form?"

Angela pulled at her hair, the anchor's question infuriating. "Are you trying to get them killed?"

"Like I said, I can't reveal any details. Doing so could get us all killed."

"Of course, of course."

Shirley pointed the remote control at the TV and muted it. "I'm sorry, I just can't listen to that. These people are idiots."

Angela turned to Maggie. "Is this where our men are?"

Maggie's chest tightened. She was the only one in the room who knew the truth, and the only reason she knew that was because of her position. Shirley saved her. "Don't ask her that. She's not allowed to tell us even if she knew."

Angela sighed. "I'm sorry. You're right. I shouldn't have put you in that position. It's just so frustrating. I always knew Niner was Delta, but that never scared me. If anything, it excited me. It made him more interesting. But once I officially knew the truth and realized how compartmentalized everything is, it…" Her shoulders slumped. "It's just so frustrating. Why can't we know?"

"Loose lips sink ships," said Vanessa. "Right now, I think we have to assume our men are in the thick of this just like they have been a hundred times before. They made it out then, they'll make it out now."

Shirley frowned. "Sweets didn't." Her eyes shot wide and her jaw dropped. She held up her hands. "Oh God, I'm so sorry. I shouldn't have said that."

Maggie patted her leg. "It's okay. We were all thinking the same thing." She took Shirley's hand then reached out for Vanessa's. "I think the best thing we can do right now is pray and hope that God listens."

Approaching Presidential Motorcade

Mexico City, Mexico

Dawson and Niner squeezed off disciplined rounds while hanging out the door of the Black Hawk, eliminating targets of opportunity as they made their final approach. The same was happening from the other three choppers. There would be no hiding the fact they were inserting. The Black Hawks were simply too loud and too visible. Their only hope was that the Apaches that continued to soften up the targets would keep any coordinated response to their arrival disorganized and muted.

"Thirty seconds!" shouted the pilot.

Dawson leaned out, peering ahead. He had given orders to insert one street over on either side of the motorcade. To attempt insertion right on top of them would be suicide. "Control, Zero-One, redirect the Apaches, over."

"Redirecting."

He spotted one of the gunships banking hard, turning its attention to the street where they would be inserting. Dawson grabbed onto one of the ropes as the Black Hawk pulled up, killing its forward momentum. Lines were tossed and he stepped out, sliding down, his M4 hammering at his shoulder as he laid down cover fire.

He hit the ground and tossed the rope aside, racing to the nearest doorway and taking cover as he surveyed the area torn apart by the Apache. He continued with the suppression fire as more of his team joined him on the ground. The Black Hawk banked away, its own guns firing a barrage of departing salvos.

He activated his comms. "Alpha Zero-One, Bravo Zero-One, have your team proceed from the south end. We're taking the north, over."

"Copy that, Bravo Zero-One. Taking the south, over."

Dawson indicated with hand signals for the team, spread across both sides of the street, to proceed north. The Apaches were now on the opposite side of the building Dawson now hugged, returning their attention to the main assault on the motorcade. Someone popped out from around the corner and raised a weapon. Dawson took him out and the man dropped in a heap.

Niner, directly behind him, cursed. "That guy's wearing a police uniform."

"Yeah, I noticed that," said Dawson as he pressed forward. "I guess the intel was right. Trust no one."

"The question is, is he wearing a uniform that isn't his, or is he actually local police that switched sides?"

Atlas grunted. "Does it matter?"

Niner shrugged. "I suppose not."

Dawson reached the end of the building and peered around the corner, spotting the roadblock preventing the motorcade from proceeding. It was a fully loaded dump truck, its tires flattened. He turned back to Atlas. "We've got a dump truck, tires shot out, blocking the way." He moved aside so Atlas could take a look. "You think you can hot-wire that thing?"

"No problem. That thing's old school."

"Good. Then that's your job. Niner, cover him." He glanced over his shoulder at Red, half the team on the other side of the street. "Hold this intersection while we clear the motorcade!"

Red gave a thumbs-up. "Roger that!"

Dawson activated his comms. "Charlie Zero-One, Bravo Zero-One, what's your status, over?"

The Charlie team lead replied. "Charlie and Foxtrot Teams in position. Standing by for your orders."

"Copy that, Charlie Zero-One. We're proceeding from the north end of the intersection now, then sweeping south on the west side of the motorcade. Have your team come in from the south, sweeping north on the east side on my mark. Watch for Alpha Team."

"Copy that, Bravo Zero-One. Awaiting your order."

Dawson turned to the others. "Shoot anything with a gun unless it's wearing a business suit. Chances are, that poor bastard is Secret Service. Watch your arcs. Friendlies will be coming up from the south on both sides of the street. And watch the windows and rooftops." He checked his weapon. "Control, Bravo Zero-One. Tell the Apaches to start clearing the road ahead. We're beginning our assault now, over."

"Copy that, Zero-One. Redirecting air support now."

"Ground Team, Bravo Zero-One. Execute! Execute! Execute!" Dawson charged around the corner, the others following, spreading out across the road as Red's team secured the intersection so there would be no surprises from behind them. Dawson sprinted toward the roadblock, his M4 raised high, scanning for any targets, but spotting none for the moment, most of the enemy either dead or hiding from the Apaches.

Gunfire rattled around the corner at the far end of the street, the distinctive sound of M4s engaging the enemy a sign this fight was far from over. He activated his comms. "This is Bravo Zero-One to Secret Service teams. Friendlies entering your perimeter from north and south, over."

His comms squawked. "This is Hotel leader. Friendlies entering from north and south."

A string of acknowledgments echoed in Dawson's ear as he advanced swiftly but cautiously. Jimmy fired from his left, two shots, then Niner did the same. Dawson reached the corner then picked off a shooter on a nearby rooftop. He peered around the corner and found the president's motorcade completely boxed in. He glanced over his shoulder to see Atlas and Niner already at the dump truck, the big man climbing inside as Niner provided cover while the Apaches continued their reign of destruction farther to the north.

Dawson signaled for the others to proceed to the south as he headed for The Beast, the nickname given to the president's armored limousine. It was flanked by four SUVs, all of them shot to hell. "Friendly approaching!" he shouted as he rounded one of the escorts, revealing

The Beast for the first time. It was pockmarked from small arms fire, but its tires appeared intact. He took a knee by the driver's window. "Is this thing still mobile?"

"Yes sir!" shouted the driver. "You just need to clear me a path!"

"We're working on it." As if to prove his point, the engine of the dump truck roared to life.

A passenger window rolled down on one of the SUVs to his left. "What's the plan?" asked the suit as gunfire continued on both sides of the streets. Dawson recognized him as Special Agent Dick Carlyle, the Secret Service team leader.

Dawson joined him. "The hostiles are regrouping now that the Apaches can't provide air cover without risking hitting our own people. First thing is to get you guys out of this kill box they've set up. As soon as that dump truck is out of the way, proceed north as far as you can."

"Some of these vehicles are no longer operational."

"Identify them, get them out of the way, and transfer the occupants to the other vehicles. I don't care if we have to stack them to the rafters. Nobody gets left behind."

"What about you guys?"

Dawson kicked the running board below the man's window. "That's why they invented these."

Carlyle laughed. "Better you than me."

Dawson returned to The Beast, taking a knee once again by the driver's window. "What's the status on our VIPs?"

"Everyone inside is okay. The president and prime minister both wish to convey their thanks for your assistance, and hope you'll forgive them for not lowering the window to deliver it in person."

Dawson chuckled. "Tell them they're forgiven and to hang tight. We'll have them outta here soon."

The engine of the dump truck protested as Atlas attempted to roll it away, but the flat tires and the heavy load were proving too much. Dawson placed a hand to his mouth. "Dump the load!" he shouted. Atlas gave a thumbs-up and the back of the massive piece of equipment tipped up, the load of sand dumping out onto the road. Dawson winced, praying the road was wide enough for the motorcade to get around the pile of sand. It should be, as long as Atlas dumped most of it in place. The big man appeared to know what he was doing, keeping the truck stationary until the dump box was fully raised.

Heavy fire from Red's position had Dawson activating his comms. "Zero-Two, Zero-One, report, over."

"Dealing with two technicals. Stand by."

An explosion erupted, followed moments later by a second, the gunfire settling.

"Threats neutralized. We had to use confiscated RPGs to take them out. We've gotta get outta here sooner rather than later. It looks like they're beginning to get more organized, over."

Dawson checked Atlas' progress, the muscled warrior jerking forward, slowly guiding the mobile roadblock out of the way, the last of the box's contents dumping onto the road. Weapons fire rang out, pinging off the dump truck. Atlas ducked and Niner opened fire on multiple targets as Dawson rushed forward to join him.

"Zero-Two, Zero-One, we're about to start rolling. Rally near the dump truck, over."

"Copy that," replied Red.

"This is Bravo Zero-One. We've cleared the roadblock. All vehicles proceed."

Atlas hopped out of the dump truck the moment it was clear of the intersection then joined Niner and Dawson as they engaged targets ahead.

Dawson searched his scope, not spotting any targets. "Clear!"

Niner and Atlas echoed his call. Dawson turned, pointing at the lead SUV, then jerked his thumb toward the now-cleared roadway. "Let's go! Let's go!" he shouted and the driver gave a thumbs-up, the SUV creeping forward through the scattered debris then over a small load of sand. A second followed then two more before The Beast finally moved.

"This is Bravo Zero-One. Everyone, grab a ride. We're not slowing for anything. Watch the rooftops and windows. Take out anything with a gun that's pointed in our direction, over." Dawson hopped onto the passenger-side running board of the lead SUV, holding on to the roof rack, his M4 ready to engage. Niner and Atlas did the same as they slowly picked up speed. "Control, Zero-One, report."

A voice he recognized from previous ops, but didn't know the name of who it belonged to, replied, Clancy obviously doing something more important. "The route ahead is clear for about one mile. However, we have another roadblock set up. It looks like multiple cars rolled onto their sides. You're not going to be driving out of there."

"Is there an alternate route?"

"Negative. There are concrete barriers blocking all access to the route you're on, and they're bolted to the ground."

Dawson cursed. "Scan the area. Is there any type of bulldozer, front-end loader, anything that we can use, some piece of construction equipment?"

"Stand by, Zero-One."

A shot rang out and Dawson caught a round to the right shoulder. He grunted in pain as he fell off the running board and tumbled onto the ground, the SUV behind him screeching to a halt, its front bumper missing his head by inches. He lay flat on his back, staring up at the heavens.

You're gonna have to do better than that if you want to take me out of this fight.

Belme Residence, West Luzon Drive

Fort Liberty, North Carolina

Maggie gasped as a man they had all agreed was her husband, fell to the ground, apparently shot. She sprang to her feet. "Does anybody see him?"

Heads shook around the room as everyone leaned closer, an SUV blocking the view. Maggie collapsed back onto the couch, biting a knuckle as tears pooled.

"Look!" cried Shirley, pointing.

Maggie wiped her eyes dry and blinked rapidly in an attempt to clear them, and she smiled as Dawson stood, giving a thumbs-up to his men before hopping on the running board of the vehicle that had almost hit him. He slapped a hand on the roof and the convoy was underway once again.

Vanessa grinned at her. "Atlas always said BD was bulletproof."

Maggie smiled weakly. "I don't know about that, but if he's got nine lives, he just used one of them."

"From the stories I've heard, he's got ninety-nine. They all do. God is definitely on their side." Vanessa pointed at the screen, a map appearing on the right side indicating where the news channel believed the motorcade was, and where it was heading. "How long would it take us to get to Atlanta?"

"Why?" asked Shirley.

"Because that's where CNN headquarters is. I think it's time to go and shoot stupid."

Maggie was gripped with rage at how irresponsible the news channel was being. They had flipped through all the channels and it appeared the CNN crew was the only one that had managed to escape with the convoy, so they had an exclusive and were taking full advantage of that. But it was one thing to show live coverage. It was another to tell the enemy exactly where the motorcade was, and where it was heading.

She grabbed the phone and dialed the Unit, getting the switchboard. "This is Maggie Dawson. Is Colonel Clancy available?"

"Sorry, Maggie. He's in the ops center."

She had figured he would be. "Can you get a message to him?"

"I can try."

"Tell him to have somebody in Washington call in an airstrike on CNN headquarters, because if they don't stop broadcasting where our guys are, I'm getting on a plane and putting an end to it myself."

"Yeah, I just saw that myself. Unbelievable. I'll get him the message. Do you want me to clean it up at all?"

"No."

"Understood."

Maggie hung up.

"Do you think that'll work?" asked Angela.

"Nope, but at least I feel better."

Shirley squeezed her hand. "You did everything you could. If the colonel gets the message, he'll make a call. We don't want Washington controlling the press, but it doesn't hurt sometimes to remind these morons that there's such a thing as responsible journalism."

"Amen."

Crash Site

Mexico City, Mexico

Master Warrant Officer Cyril Dwyer slid down the rope, his C8-SFW assault rifle at the ready as he surveyed the area. Two of the downed helicopters were within sight at opposite ends of the street, the third a couple of hundred yards away, his second team already inserting.

He hit the ground and tossed the rope aside, rushing toward the closest downed chopper as he kept a wary eye out for hostiles. The Black Hawk that had brought them rose, his team delivered into the thick of things, the helicopter crew's job finished. They were sitting ducks if they remained in the area, and he just prayed they made it back to base unscathed.

Using hand signals, he ordered his men to secure the area while he and MWO Bren Hynes, their most experienced medic, picked their way through the wreckage. The airframe was smoldering, though it hadn't yet caught fire, but things could change in a heartbeat.

"Friendlies approaching!" he shouted.

"Acknowledged!" called someone from inside.

Dwyer slung his weapon and pulled himself inside the hold, teetering on a precarious angle. He spotted two of the crew, one holding his leg, the other prone on the deck.

"Status?" asked Dwyer as Hynes scrambled over to the prone man.

"I've got a broken leg, but other than that, I'm fine. I don't know about Peters. He's got a pulse but he's out cold. Captain, you still kicking?"

A voice from the cockpit replied. "I don't know about kicking, but I'm still breathing."

Dwyer made his way past Hynes and poked his head into the cockpit to see the copilot with a bleeding forehead but conscious, the pilot gripping both his upper legs, the console shoved against them.

"What's your status?"

The copilot continued following the book as he reported. "We were shot down, probably by a Stinger, as you already know. I've been able to do a full shutdown so hopefully we won't be exploding." He pressed a button and held his hands up. "I've just destroyed the last of the classified equipment." He turned to the pilot. "Now we just need to get you the hell out of here."

"I don't know how the hell we're going to manage that," winced the pilot. "My legs are stuck."

Dwyer glanced over his shoulder at Hynes, still working on the unconscious man. "How's he look?"

"He's out cold. He's got one hell of a tennis ball forming on his head. Probably a concussion. He needs medical attention stat before the swelling gets too bad and starts to cause some damage."

"Is he safe to move?"

"I think so. It doesn't look like any broken bones."

"Then get him outside and clear of the chopper, then come back and get a splint on that broken leg. I'm going to try to free our pilot."

"You got it." Hynes picked up the unconscious man and stepped through the side door of the chopper and out of sight.

Dwyer examined the pilot's seat. It was bolted in place, already as far back as it could go. There was no simple adjustment to get the man out. They would need leverage.

"Friendly approaching!"

"Acknowledged!" Dwyer turned to see Hynes stepping inside and he cocked an eyebrow at the sight of a civilian, a local.

"Hola. Can I help?" asked the man, his accent thick but his English good.

Dwyer took a chance and pointed at the seat. "This man is trapped. We need to get him out."

The local crawled inside on his hands and knees then peered at the bolts holding the chair in place. "I'll be back." He scrambled outside, shouting something as Hynes tended to the broken leg.

Dwyer climbed back into the cockpit. "We might have some friendly locals, so you just sit tight."

The pilot eyeballed him. "Sit tight. Are you trying to be funny?"

Dwyer laughed. "I don't think I've ever been accused of having a sense of humor."

"That makes two of us. According to my kids, my dad jokes are not funny."

Dwyer patted the man on the shoulder then turned his attention to the copilot. "How are you feeling?"

"Splitting headache, but I'm guessing I'll live."

"Okay, let's get you out of here."

"I'm not leaving the captain."

"Bullshit," replied the pilot. "Get the hell out of here. This thing could still go up, and if you get yourself killed because you're hanging around with me, I'm going to be pissed and have to kill you myself again. Get out, I'll be fine. That's an order."

The copilot frowned then sighed. "Fine."

Dwyer helped the man out of his seat then into the tilted cabin and onto the ground. The local and another man jogged up, carrying toolboxes.

"We'll get him out, don't worry."

Dwyer gave them a thumbs-up and helped Hynes carry the crewmember with the broken leg to the other side of the road. They placed him down gently. "Radio it in. Let them know what to expect."

"Yes, sir."

Dwyer returned to the chopper to find the two locals unbolting the seat, making quick work of it. He hung back, not wanting to get in the way as Hynes reported the medical situation to Control. He cursed at the ETA. The convoy sent to get them was fifteen minutes out, if not worse.

The streets were gridlocked, the cartels having successfully created a nightmare.

But that was the next problem. First, was getting everybody clear of the choppers.

"Sierra Zero-Two, Sierra Leader, what's your status, over?"

"We've got three clear, one dead, over."

Dwyer frowned. One dead. He had hoped they might get lucky, but that had just been wishful thinking. Helicopter crashes were violent, especially when it was a result of being shot out of the air. "Copy that. Are the three survivors mobile, over?"

"Affirmative."

"Then bring everybody to our position. We'll consolidate here, over."

"Copy that. Bringing them now. Out."

"Tango Leader, this is Sierra Leader. What's your status, over?"

Tango Leader responded, his voice a little higher-pitched than normal, indicating a problem. "Tango Leader here. We've secured the chopper. Four survivors, one seriously wounded. We came under heavy fire but we managed to take out the targets. I don't know how secure we are here, over."

"Copy that. Are your survivors mobile, over?"

"We'll have to carry one of them out. The others can make it on their own."

"Copy that. Fall back to our position. We're secure here for the moment."

"Roger that. We're on our way. Tango Leader, out."

Cries of triumph from the locals had Dwyer returning his attention to the extraction operation underway. The two men gently pulled the seat back, free of its bolts, and the pilot screamed in agony as his legs were released.

Hynes rushed inside and Dwyer stepped out of the way as the medic examined the pilot's legs. "I was afraid of this. He might have compartment syndrome. We need to get him proper medical attention or he's going to lose his legs."

"Nuts to that," said the pilot. "There's no effing way I'm losing my legs."

Hynes eyed him. "We might not have a choice, sir."

The pilot grabbed Hynes by the vest. "I'm not losing my legs, you hear me?"

"I hear you." Hynes turned to Dwyer. "We've got to get out of here. We can't wait for the extraction team. This guy's gonna lose his legs, and we've got one out there whose brain is swelling as we speak."

Dwyer nodded. "Understood. Get him out and clear." He stepped outside as Hynes and the locals helped the pilot, and activated his comms. "Control, Sierra Leader. What's the status on the extraction, over."

"Ten minutes out, but they're reporting a roadblock that could delay them. They're attempting to find another route to your position, over."

"I've got at least two that aren't going to last that long. Is there any chance of getting a helo in here to extract them, over?"

"Negative. There's no safe LZ near you."

Two Apaches thundered overhead, heading toward gunfire that rattled in the distance.

"What about the Apaches?" he asked.

"Those only hold two and both seats are occupied," replied Control.

"I'm well aware of that. I'm looking for volunteers. An Apache only needs a pilot and they need a hell of a lot less area to land in. We just need to get the wounded out, the rest of us can wait."

"Stand by, Sierra Leader."

Dwyer turned to see the pilot being carried across the street in his seat. The two locals placed him gently on the ground and Hynes went to work, but he gave him a look, shaking his head slightly. Good men were going to die, and he had to find a way to prevent that.

Presidential Motorcade

Mexico City, Mexico

Florencia whimpered as they finally moved forward. Everyone continued to stay low, and she no longer only had Anderson weighing her down, but two new occupants had joined them, their own car shot to hell. She thought she had been through too much to bear, but when the door had opened, the two arrivals had dived in, sobbing uncontrollably. It was obvious things had been much worse for some of the others. She could still hear gunfire in the distance, and somebody cried out as there was a loud thud just on the other side of her door and the whole car rocked.

"What the hell was that?" she cried.

"Just one of the Special Forces hitching a ride," replied the driver. "If he fires his weapon, it's gonna be loud, so just be prepared for that. It's not that things got any worse, it's just that the good guys are closer."

"Is it over?" asked Anderson. "We're moving now. Does that mean it's over?"

"Not by a long shot. It's a seven-mile trip and we've only done a mile of it. Control indicates another roadblock ahead, but we've got Special Forces with us now and air support. We're gonna make it. It's just a matter of time."

Heavy gunfire ahead had Florencia pressing her hands against her ears in a futile attempt to block out reality.

Please, God, get us through this.

The Unit

Fort Liberty, North Carolina

Clancy hung up the phone, Washington constantly interrupting demanding updates, it seemed, every two minutes. "Any luck finding construction equipment?"

"Yes, sir," replied the ops center controller. "There's a construction site two streets over that has heavy equipment."

"Do they have what we need?"

"Yes, sir."

"Is it operational?"

"Sir?"

"Is there anyone there to give them the keys?"

"Oh, just a second." The controller tapped at her keyboard, staring at one of her screens, then gave a thumbs-up. "Twenty minutes ago, satellite shows that work was underway at the site."

"Good. Let BD know."

"Yes, sir."

A throat cleared behind him and he turned to see a corporal standing there. "What is it, Corporal?"

The young man handed him a folded piece of paper. "A message from the switchboard, sir."

Clancy's eyes narrowed as he took the page. "Why didn't it come through regular channels?"

"I was told it was of a personal nature."

Clancy unfolded the page and his eyebrows shot up.

Maggie Dawson recommends airstrike on CNN headquarters in Atlanta.

Clancy spun toward the wall to his left, half a dozen screens showing various news channels. He cursed at the split screen, the left showing live footage from the battle, the right showing a map, giving the exact location of his men with a projected route. "You have got to be kidding me." He pointed at one of his people. "Get me the White House Press Secretary, now!"

Presidential Motorcade

Mexico City, Mexico

Aynslee Kai ducked as more gunfire rang out. She had been under fire before, most recently in Myanmar, and had hoped to never repeat the experience. Yet, here she was, only weeks later under fire once again. She recognized some of the Special Forces as those she had encountered the last time, not from their faces, which were mostly covered, but from their mannerisms and body shapes. The man who had moved the dump truck was clearly Atlas, and his diminutive partner had to be Niner. The man who appeared in control had the confident, unmistakable swagger of Dawson.

If these were the men sent to save them, she had no doubt they would succeed or they would die trying. These were the type of men who never gave up, and for the moment, with the motorcade underway again, her confidence was slowly returning.

Neville Roy pointed ahead as he refocused his camera. "Something's going on."

Aynslee rose slightly and peered over the dashboard to see several of the Delta team sprinting down a side street. "I wonder what the hell that's all about."

"I don't know, but I'd love to be following them."

She regarded her cameraman. "You're a special kind of lunatic, aren't you?"

"You know it, girl."

The Secret Service agent driving eyeballed them both. "If either of you leaves this car, I'm shooting you myself."

Aynslee grinned at Roy. "I guess that settles that."

Atlanta chirped in her ear. "We're ready to go live again, Aynslee."

"Copy that, Chuck. We just got some footage of some of the Special Forces breaking off. Make sure you don't air that. I don't want anything going live that puts these people at risk." There was a pause and Aynslee tensed. "Please tell me you've been vetting the footage."

"Sorry, Aynslee. I know I said we would, but I was overruled. We've been broadcasting you live."

She cursed. "You're supposed to filter out anything that could identify individuals or where we were. You're telling me you haven't been doing that?"

"No. It looks like we've got an exclusive here. Nobody in the world is covering this, so the brain trust said to stop filtering, put everything out live."

Aynslee pulled out her phone and brought up the CNN website, growling in rage at the map on the homepage. "You guys put up a map with our location and our predicted route? You tell those sons of bitches that anyone who dies, the blood's on their hands, and that I'll be naming names to these Special Forces guys who just might wanna pay Atlanta a visit when this is all over. You morons better pray nobody gets killed because you wanted ratings."

"I understand you're angry, Aynslee…Just a second. What is it?"

A voice in the background had Aynslee smiling. "It's the White House Press Secretary."

"What's she want?"

"She wants to know how long CNN has been working for the drug cartels."

"What?"

"She says since CNN is actively participating in attempting to kill the President of the United States, she's assuming we must be working for the cartels."

Aynslee grinned at Roy, privy to the conversation with his own earpiece.

"Aynslee, I've gotta take this call."

"I guess you do."

"Are you ready to go live?"

"Nope. There'll be nothing else coming out of Mexico City until you guys start being responsible." She cut off the call as Roy lowered his camera.

"So, we're not shooting?"

"No, no, keep shooting. Just make sure we're not transmitting anything. We can piece things together after the fact."

"You know we could get fired."

She shrugged. "Getting fired for my principles is something I can live with." She pointed out the window. "Now, get that camera rolling. I don't wanna miss a thing. We are still reporters, after all."

Approaching the Construction Site

Mexico City, Mexico

Niner led the way down the side street, Atlas directly behind him, Spock and Jimmy on the opposite side of the road. Control indicated there was heavy equipment less than half a mile from their current position. If they could commandeer a dozer, they could blast through any barriers ahead of them. It would be slow going because these things weren't known for speed, but anything was better than a dead stop, which is what the motorcade faced directly ahead.

A dozer would give them options. They could move blockages set up by the enemy, but they could also move the concrete barriers set up by the Mexican authorities that had served their purpose in keeping traffic off the road, but had also had the unintended consequence of boxing them in.

He reached the next street and stopped, peering around the corner. He spotted two police officers standing by their cruiser. He turned to the others. "Two uniformed police at a cruiser. Don't shoot unless they raise their weapons." Thumbs-up from the others acknowledged his order. "Cover me."

He sprinted across the road, keeping his eyes on the two policemen. One of them pointed and the other spun around. The first raised his weapon then stopped as the other reached out and shoved the muzzle to the ground.

"Americanos?" asked the second, and Niner gave a thumbs-up.

The man waved them through. "Good luck, amigos."

Niner cleared the intersection then indicated for the others to follow as he covered the two officers just in case they were luring them out, but it appeared they weren't. Not all of Mexico's police force was corrupt today.

"One-One, Control, next intersection on your left, you'll see the construction site, over."

"Copy that, Control," acknowledged Niner.

"One-One, Zero-One, we're approaching the next barricade. What's your status, over."

Niner sprinted toward the next intersection, letting the others cover him, sensing the urgency in Dawson's voice. "Coming up on the construction site now. Stand by, over." Niner reached the corner, finding it clear, and spotting exactly what they needed on the opposite side of the road.

A massive front loader parked at the bottom of what would eventually be the parking levels of a new building.

The heavy footfalls of Atlas joined him, and Niner pointed. "You think you can get that beast running?"

Atlas indicated the exhaust gently puffing away. "She's already running. Looks like whoever was manning her abandoned it as soon as the gunfire started."

"Okay, get in there. Make sure she's fueled up. We're probably gonna need to run her the entire way to the airport."

"Copy that."

Niner and Atlas crossed the intersection and Atlas ran down the ramp dug into the pit. Niner pointed at Spock and Jimmy. "Cover the intersection."

"Copy that."

Niner took a knee, quickly scanning the construction site, watching for any hostiles, as Atlas climbed into the cab of the huge piece of equipment. The engine roared and the blade lifted off the ground. It tilted forward, spilling its contents, before Atlas had the massive machine chugging toward the ramp.

Niner activated his comms. "Zero-One, One-One, we've got a front loader. I repeat, we've got a front loader." He ran down the ramp then hopped up on the side of the loader. He yanked open the door. "How's the fuel?"

"Three-quarters of a tank."

"Let's hope that's enough. Something tells me this thing doesn't get very good mileage."

"Probably not." They crested the ramp, the tracked beast handling like a tank, continuing at an upward angle until its center of mass passed the tipping point. The huge piece of equipment bounced down onto the road and Niner beckoned Spock and Jimmy. They sprinted toward the machine, climbing on as he contacted Control.

"Control, One-One, what's our best route for getting to that next blockade, keeping in mind there's no way this thing is getting around that motorcade, over."

"One-One, Control. Turn to your right and take the road parallel to the evac route. It looks clear the entire way. You should then be able to cut over and clear the blockage."

Niner indicated the advised direction and Atlas expertly had them heading at full speed moments later. Unfortunately, full speed was a crawl. "Control, One-One, at our current speed, what's our ETA to target?"

"We estimate seven minutes."

Niner groaned.

Might as well be seven hours.

"Zero-One, One-One, ETA seven minutes your position. We'll be coming up from behind the barricade, over."

"Copy that, One-One. We'll hold this position as long as we can. If there's any way to shave some time off that ETA, do it. Seconds are gonna matter here, over."

"Copy that, Zero-One. We'll do our best. If you want, I can send two of our team ahead to assist. It's literally faster on foot, over."

"Negative, One-One. You need them for cover. If that loader doesn't arrive, then this shit show turns into a Charlie Foxtrot, over."

"Copy that, Zero-One. Cavalry's on the way." Niner leaned into the cabin. "Is there anything you can do to speed this thing up a bit?"

Atlas shook his head. "I've already got it cranked. This is as good as it gets. They're just gonna have to hold out those seven minutes."

Crash Site

Mexico City, Mexico

Dwyer squeezed the trigger twice, taking out a hostile at the far end of the street. They were drawing attention, their enemy converging on the area, no doubt eager to get their hands on prisoners that could be used in exchange for the release of the drug lords taken several days ago.

An Apache raced down the street, opening fire then pulling up rapidly and dropping to the ground, landing with a bounce. The canopy popped open and the gunner climbed out.

Dwyer turned to Hynes. "Who's first?"

"The captain. There's nothing I can do for him here."

The injured pilot vehemently shook his head. "Bullshit. My crew goes first."

"If we don't get you immediate medical attention, not only are you going to lose those legs, you're going to lose your life."

“Don’t care. You said Peters has swelling on the brain. You take him first.”

Dwyer pointed at the still-unconscious man. “We don’t have time to argue. Get him in the chopper.”

“Yes, sir,” said Hynes, none too pleased. Hynes and the Apache gunner helped Peters into the front seat of the Apache then closed the canopy before rushing clear of the rotors. The gunship lifted off and banked away, gunfire from around the area chasing it. The pilot kept low between the buildings, and the airframe tilted forward as it gained speed while a second Apache made a strafing run then began to land.

Hynes turned to the captain. “Your turn.”

“No, take the lieutenant.”

The copilot nixed that idea. “No effing way, Captain. I just have a bump on my head. You’re next.”

Hynes and one of the other team members hauled the pilot to his feet. “He’s right, Captain. You’re next.”

The man winced as he was carried toward the chopper as it landed, and he glared at his copilot. “If something happens to you, I’m going to be pissed.”

The copilot grinned. “That’ll make two of us.”

Dwyer and the others continued to provide cover as the pilot was loaded into the gunner’s seat. The Apache departed moments later and Dwyer breathed a relieved sigh as the first reported it was clear of the area.

“Friendlies approaching from the east!”

Dwyer turned to see Tango Team finally joining them from the third chopper. Three crewmembers appeared battered and bruised, but were mobile. The fourth was on a stretcher. "What's his status?"

"Not good. He needs immediate evac."

"Copy that." Dwyer activated his comms. "Control, Sierra Leader. We need one more Apache for an emergency evac, over."

"Copy that, Sierra Leader. Stand by."

Dwyer turned to the two Apache gunners that had volunteered their seats to save their brothers-in-arms. "Are you armed?"

One of them smacked his holster. "Side arms only."

Dwyer regarded them. "Do you guys actually know how to shoot those things, or are they for show?"

The man chuckled. "We're trained, but something tells me we're novices compared to you guys."

"I'm sure you'll do fine."

Dwyer's comms squawked. "Sierra Leader, Control. Third Apache en route, ETA sixty seconds. Satellite is showing hostiles converging on the area, over."

"ETA on the extraction team?"

"Six minutes at best."

"Copy that, Control. Six minutes. Sierra Leader, out."

"Technical, west side!"

Dwyer spun to see a Nissan pickup truck roll into the intersection, a .50 cal loaded in the back manned by two hostiles. He cursed. "We don't have six minutes."

Presidential Motorcade

Mexico City, Mexico

Dawson reloaded his M4 and resumed fire as the motorcade continued to creep forward. They had barely covered half a mile after being inserted. Enemy opposition was stiffening the longer they were delayed, and the amount of debris scattered on the road wasn't helping. The SUVs and cars could get around easily enough. It was The Beast that was the problem. It was too big.

Dawson sprinted ahead and hopped on the running board of the vehicle with the head of the secret service team, Special Agent Carlyle. He didn't want what he was about to say to go out over the comms. Carlyle, sitting in the passenger seat with his window down as he fired his Glock at targets of opportunity, withdrew his weapon as Dawson leaned in.

"When are your boys getting here with that loader? I can see that barricade from here."

Dawson peered ahead, confirming Carlyle's concern. "Should be here in about three minutes, but we've got another problem."

"What's that?"

"They've moved shit into this road all along the route, and trying to get off the route is next to impossible. It's gridlock out there."

"Tell me something I don't know, Sergeant Major."

"We've gotta get the president out of The Beast."

Carlyle gave him an incredulous look. "Are you nuts? That's the only thing keeping him alive."

"No, sir. It's the thing that's gonna get us all killed. Get him into one of these up-armored SUVs and we can double or triple our speed easily. Right now, we've got no options. That thing's turning radius is shit. We need to abandon that thing so we can increase our mobility."

Carlyle chewed his cheek for a moment as he stared ahead at the barrier that continued to grow closer. He pointed ahead, a decision made, at least for the moment. "Unless your boys can clear that, it doesn't matter what he's driving in. Let's keep him in there for now, and when we're clear of that barricade ahead, I'll consider it."

"Very well. I recommend you advise them to prepare for your contingency that I know you already have in place." Dawson tapped his earpiece. "Control tells me it's a disaster the entire route. Whatever the hell the cartels are up to, they're trying to delay us. My guess is so they can position for one final assault."

A frown creased Carlyle's face. "You think they intend to kill the president?"

"You better hope that's what they intend, because if they capture him, the entire world will be watching as they torture him until they get what they want."

Crash Site

Mexico City, Mexico

Dwyer smiled as the Apache launched two rockets, the technical that had them pinned down bursting in flames. Half a dozen of his men rushed forward to resecure the intersection, hostiles closing in on all sides now. The Apache pulled up sharply then banked to the left, dropping back down low and racing over their heads before pulling up again, killing its forward momentum and dropping to the ground.

The third seriously injured crewmember was loaded in and the Apache was gone moments later. Dwyer took cover behind an abandoned car and flipped open the cover on his tactical computer. The extraction team with armored vehicles was five minutes out and were coming in from the north. Hostiles were converging on the area, the smoldering wreckage of the crashed choppers beacons that could be seen for miles.

"Control, Sierra Leader. What's it look like to the north, over."

"You've got hostiles coming in on all streets, but it's no worse than any other direction, over."

Dwyer made a decision that he hoped he wouldn't regret. "Copy that, Control. We're going to move north toward the extraction team and away from the crash sites. Hopefully, that'll reduce the number of hostiles we're going to be dealing with, over."

"Acknowledged, Sierra Leader. Good luck, over."

"This is Sierra Leader. We're going to head north toward the extraction team. Everybody fall back to the main intersection and prepare the rescued for immediate evac, over."

Acknowledgments came in over his earpiece as he pointed at Hynes. "Pick whoever you need. Get the flight crews ready. We're leaving in sixty seconds."

"Copy that."

The rescued crews all rose, some swifter than others, as Hynes coordinated their evac. Dwyer headed for the main intersection where the Apaches had been landing. He peered around the corner in the direction they were about to head. Everything appeared clear for the moment, but that could change in a split second. His intention was to move one intersection at a time. They just had to put some distance between them and the wreckage, because in the next couple of minutes, scores of hostiles threatened to overwhelm them.

"We're ready!" shouted Hynes.

Dwyer didn't bother looking, instead surging forward. "Let's go!" He sprinted forward with the bulk of his team spread out on either side of the street, the second JTF 2 unit covering the rear, the wounded between.

He monitored his arc and swung his weapon as a door opened. A local poked her head out and pointed across the street, then disappeared back inside.

Dwyer aimed toward the alleyway the woman had indicated, then motioned for two of his men to follow as he hugged one side of the street, getting a better angle on the alleyway on the opposite side. A police officer stepped out, his weapon raised, and Dwyer took him out. Another appeared and he squeezed the trigger again, the man dropping in a heap.

It had him wondering if there were any real police officers left in the city. He refused to believe so many were crooked and fighting for the wrong side. It had to be that the cartels had a large number of fake uniforms.

He continued forward, covering the alleyway, and as he reached it, confirmed it was now clear. He continued onward, reaching the next intersection, and held up. He peered around the corner. Two men ran across the street to the east, carrying assault rifles, heading toward the crash site. He held up a fist indicating for everyone to hold while he waited for them to clear. They disappeared out of sight and he sprinted across the street and took up a covering position as his team secured the intersection. He indicated for several of his men to continue forward as the flight crew reached the intersection.

An engine revved and he cursed as another technical raced toward the crash site. He indicated for everyone to hold, then the moment the technical cleared the intersection and was out of sight, he beckoned the flight crew and those helping them to proceed. Hynes led the way and the group slowly inched their way forward, the cluster sticking together, no one going faster than the slowest man. It was honorable but frustrating to watch. A dozen men grouped together was a lot more obvious than three or four, and right now, anyone could round a corner at any moment and phone in what was happening.

What felt like an eternity but was only seconds finally ended as the last cleared the open road, everyone once again hugging the side of a building. He turned to the survivors. "Next intersection, everyone crosses as fast as you can. Don't wait for the slow man. You just make a bigger, more obvious target. I understand you want to support your crewmates, but trust us, we'll take care of them."

Heads bobbed, acknowledging the reality of their situation.

"Good. Then let's get a move on."

Engines roared and Hynes cursed, jerking his chin toward the far end of the block they were now on. Dwyer spun to find two technicals entering the intersection, blocking them off.

"Check your six!" warned one of his team and he turned to see another technical and half a dozen hostiles on foot in the intersection where the Apaches had previously landed only minutes ago.

They had been found.

En Route to Motorcade

Mexico City, Mexico

Niner, perched in the scoop of the loader, pressed into one corner, Spock in the other, as Atlas continued to guide them toward the roadblock preventing the motorcade from proceeding. He fired two more rounds, taking out another hostile. The closer they got to the scene, the heavier the resistance. Jimmy was lying on the roof, prone, covering their sixes. They were only a couple of minutes out. One more turn. But Control had indicated the way ahead was only worse.

The thunder of helicopter rotors overwhelmed the area and Niner smiled as an Apache banked around a building ahead, its cannons blazing as it shredded the ground-level facades and cars parked in front of him, eliminating at least a dozen of the opposition facing them. The Apache raced past then banked hard, pulling an impressive 180, reminding Niner of one of his favorite eighties action movies, Blue Thunder.

The Apache made a second pass, this time taking out the opposite side of the street as Atlas continued guiding them inexorably toward their destination. The Apache disappeared around another building, its rotors falling almost silent, though the gunfire continued out of sight as it cleared a path down the road they were about to take.

Niner stretched an arm out toward their turn and glanced over his shoulder at Atlas. "Next left! Next left!"

Atlas gave a thumbs-up but maintained their speed, not willing to give up even a second. More bullets pinged off the bucket they were using for cover, and Spock cursed.

"I'm beginning to get the distinct impression that somebody's unhappy about what we did the other night."

Niner gave him a look. "Ya think?"

"I do," said Spock, playing the straight man. He popped up, firing several rounds before ducking back down. "You do realize this is never going to end."

Niner fired as Atlas turned. Spock was right. The cartels had proven what they were capable of with the Night of Reckoning, but now they were proving how far they were willing to go to get what they wanted. They wanted their people released, and he couldn't see the president being willing to give in. Taking all the cartel leaders at once had been a bold and impressive move, but in hindsight, foolish. It forced all the cartels to react at once. It united them in their cause. If they had only taken one of the leaders, the other cartels might have gone to war to take over his turf. It could have caused chaos while they put a show trial on back home.

Unfortunately, what should or shouldn't have happened would be left to the historians. Those left suffering today by the bad decisions of politicians would have to figure a way out of it. If enough time passed, those filling in for their imprisoned bosses might decide they enjoyed having power, and simply leave their former chiefs to rot in prison and stand down their response. After all, violence like this wasn't good for business. But how long would that take? How many would die? How many Nights of Reckoning would there be before somebody called an end to it?

It wasn't his job to solve these problems, though it was soldiers like him left to deal with the consequences, and he had to wonder how many of his brothers and sisters-in-arms were going to die, all so someone could look tough on crime rather than dealing with the real problem. Drug dealers supplied something the customer wanted. If there were no customers wanting their product, they would go out of business. Address the reasons for the demand, then the supply would take care of itself. Unfortunately, he had no idea how to deal with the demand, and he wondered if anyone did.

Fortunately, that too wasn't his problem.

Crash Site

Mexico City, Mexico

Dwyer booted open a door. "Everybody inside!" he ordered, the survivors scrambling to execute his order as his men opened fire on what was now four technicals and twenty to thirty men opposing them. This was where they would be making their final stand by the looks of it. "Control, Sierra Leader. Where's that air support, over?"

"Sierra Leader, Control. We've got two gunships en route. ETA four minutes. Exfil convoy is two minutes out, over."

"Copy that, Control. Tell them they're coming into a hot recovery zone."

"Acknowledged, Sierra Leader, they're aware, over."

A tango entered his arc and he took him out, this one wearing a military uniform.

Hynes tapped him on the shoulder. "All the survivors are inside."

"Okay. Once that convoy gets here, I don't want a second wasted."

"You got it, boss."

Heavy sustained gunfire rattled behind them. Dwyer ignored it. If he needed to be made aware of what was going on, one of his men would inform him. His job was the intersection ahead, and preventing the hostiles from making any gains toward their position. He fired a couple more rounds, the gunner in the rear of the left most technical crouching.

It was clear from what he was seeing that the cartels had been well prepared. Pickup trucks were one thing, but .50-caliber machine guns including mounts, with time enough to rig them, was another. Not to mention the fact they had enough of them to pursue what should be a secondary target. It made him wonder what the main force at the motorcade was dealing with. He had been monitoring the comms and was well aware of the progress, or lack thereof, of the president's motorcade, and was eager to get into that battle.

An engine roared. Loud. This wasn't another pickup truck, this was a big diesel engine on a heavy piece of machinery. A rocket ripped across the cityscape from out of sight, then one of the technicals erupted in a massive explosion, tossing it into the air and on top of its partner. A French-built Mexican Army Panhard wheeled combat vehicle rolled into sight and Dwyer breathed a sigh of relief.

The rescue convoy they had been waiting for had arrived.

He turned to Hynes. "Get everyone ready."

"You got it." Hynes disappeared inside the building sheltering the survivors. Dwyer waved as the Panhard turned down their street, followed by half a dozen more. The gunner opened fire on the far end of the road, targeting the other two technicals that had engaged them, tearing them apart and sending the hostiles scrambling for cover. It continued past Dwyer's position and the second one stopped, its rear hatch dropping to the ground, two medics emerging.

"How many have you got?" asked one of them, his English near perfect.

"One dead, eight mobile with various types of injuries, plus twenty-four of my men."

"Let's get them loaded."

"Hynes, let's go!"

The door flew open and two men helped a wounded comrade out. They rounded the rear of the transport and disappeared inside, five more joining him before the medics cut off the parade. "That's it. Rest of you, get in the next one." The medics disappeared inside and the ramp closed, the Panhard turning around, repositioning for their escape as a second and third turned, dropping their rear gates.

"Let's go! Let's go! Let's go!" ordered Dwyer, and Hynes led the rest of the survivors into the rear of one of the transports. Dwyer activated his comms. "This is Sierra Leader. Everyone fall back and get inside one of the transports, over."

The teams collapsed back on the street with their rescue vehicles. Dwyer positioned himself near the rear hatch of one of them as the two teams of JTF 2 operators withdrew from the battle in an orderly fashion, filling the armored transports to capacity.

"Let's go, sir!" shouted one of the Mexican Special Forces that had just saved their asses. Dwyer gave him a curt nod and stepped inside as the ramp slowly closed and the engine surged, pulling them out of the battle.

Unfortunately, there was still a war to win.

Presidential Motorcade

Mexico City, Mexico

An Apache strafed the roadblock ahead as the motorcade once again ground to a halt. Niner's voice came in over Dawson's earpiece. "Zero-One, One-One. We're about to come around the corner. Encountering heavy resistance, over."

"Copy that, One-One. Moving to provide cover now, over." Dawson and the others advanced, sending a wall of lead toward the enemy. The front loader echoed between the buildings and the large scoop came into sight, Niner and Spock inside.

A shot rang out from overhead, ricocheting off the ground at Dawson's feet. He dove to his left, rolling before regaining a knee and taking out the gunman on the opposite rooftop. The loader was turning toward them now, Atlas behind the controls, Jimmy lying on top, firing behind them. Dawson rose, rushing past the roadblock while Spock and Niner climbed out of the bucket as Atlas lowered it.

The two men joined the rest of Bravo Team as they continued to advance, covering Atlas as the bucket hit the ground and rammed into the roadblock made of several cars and concrete barriers, and an apparent inexhaustible source of burning tires. The massive machine made quick work of the blockade and Dawson jumped on board, pointing at the road ahead. "You take the lead. Keep best possible speed. Just punch a hole big enough for The Beast."

Atlas gave him a thumbs-up. "If I can get through then it can get through. Just cover me. I'm a sitting duck in here." He tapped the window made of plastic. "This ain't transparent aluminum."

"You got it." Dawson hopped down as Atlas turned the loader around. The big man kept the blade just off the ground as the piece of construction equipment rumbled forward. Dawson indicated for his team to spread out then activated his comms. "Control, Zero-One, we need those Apaches to begin continuous strafing runs along the route ahead, over."

"Copy that, Zero-One. We've only got four in the pattern. Three were retasked for emergency medical support, but are now back in their primary role. You should start to see more active support in the next two minutes, over."

"Copy that, Control. Where are we on an alternate route?"

"No joy. The cartels have the city in gridlock."

Dawson cursed. If there was no way out of here, it meant the cartels had no intention of taking the president alive. Their intent was to kill him then disappear into the woodwork.

A burning tire rolled toward them, the man who had sent it scrambling for cover but tripping to the ground after Niner put a round in his ass. Somebody rushed from a side street and grabbed him, dragging him away, but Dawson was prepared for this, taking the man out as he signaled Red and Jagger to advance with him. This was the first chance they had at getting a prisoner. They needed to know what the cartels' intentions were, and if they got lucky, they might just get someone talkative when in pain.

He sprinted ahead, his M4 at the ready, flanked by Red and Jagger. He took a knee beside the wounded hostile, groaning in agony. "Do you speak English?"

"Go to hell."

"I'll take that as a yes." Dawson pointed back toward the motorcade, still crawling forward. "There's a medic back there with all kinds of wonderful painkillers that'll have you feeling good in about five seconds. If that sounds good to you, then all you've got to do is answer a few easy questions."

"I'm not telling you anything."

"Then I'll have my friend patch you up with no painkillers, put you on camera with the CNN crew we've got back there, and thank you personally for your assistance, then put you back on the street. What do you think your buddies are going to do then?"

The man's eyes shot wide with horror. "You wouldn't."

"I would. But if you answer my questions, I'll have you patched up, given meds, and we'll take you back to the States and put you in witness protection with a nice little pension. Your buddies will never find you.

So, what's it going to be? Skinned alive by your friends, or a cushy retirement in America?"

The man glared at him then his shoulders slumped. "Fine. What do you want to know?"

"What's your intention? Kill the president or capture him?"

"Capture him."

Dawson exchanged a surprised glance with Red, covering his left flank but close enough to hear. "If you're trying to capture him, then why the hell is there so much shooting?"

The man shrugged. "The bullets won't penetrate that car. Our job is just to slow them down until our people arrive."

"What people?"

"The ones with the really heavy weapons. The ones that can blow the shit out of all your armored vehicles as if they were made of paper."

"You have to know you'd need a tank to get into The Beast."

"We don't need to get in. We just need him to get out."

"What do you mean?"

"Have you ever boiled an egg?"

Operations Center 2, CIA Headquarters

Langley, Virginia

Leroux stared at the massive display. On the left third was a map tracking Raul Garza's tagged luggage and Sherrie's current position, along with footage from a drone and a satellite. So far, there had been no surprises. The current thinking was that they were heading toward Copper Canyon, and it made sense. It was sparsely populated with lots of hillsides to dig tunnels into and create an underground fortress that would be nearly impenetrable to ground forces.

As each hour passed, the noose tightened around Garza, the man who masterminded the Night of Reckoning, and believed to be masterminding the current mayhem in Mexico City. Eliminate him, and they might just put an end to this, at least temporarily.

The immediate focus for all departments, however, was how the hell to save the president's life. Delta was on the ground and were second to none in their abilities, but there was only so much they could do against such overwhelming odds. It was as if the cartels had known exactly where the president would be headed, but had covered all their bases just in case.

They had been prepared for helicopters, using the Stingers to take out the three decoys launched as soon as the attack had begun. Three escape routes had been created, all blocked off ahead of time, the two alternates the targets of the initial explosions, the roadways taken out, forcing the president's motorcade to use the route they were now trapped on. It had been left cleared just enough to let them get too far from the palace to turn back, more explosions destroying the roadway behind them, and it was still open ahead all the way to the airport except for roadblocks that could be pushed aside.

Everything was temporary, as if they wanted them to keep moving forward.

There had to be somebody on the inside. Somebody in the know. Very few people knew the actual route that would be used for the president's escape. Two were alternates, plus there were several decoy routes set up they had no intention of using. Someone had known to ignore the decoys, blow up the alternates, and leave the preferred route open.

He couldn't see it being anyone on the American or Canadian sides. It had to be someone within the Mexican security apparatus. But who? And at the moment, did it matter? This had been going on for less than half an hour, and already the reaction was swift. The Beast had state-of-the-art communications equipment, and the president was fully informed of what was going on. He had approved additional forces. The Air Force had already scrambled F-35s, more attack helicopters, an AWACS, and an AC-130 gunship that could pulverize anything once it got over the area.

Unfortunately, with the exception of the F-35s, everything was over an hour out.

Washington had already informed the Mexicans what was coming and that if they wanted to minimize civilian casualties, they would order everyone in the immediate vicinity of the motorcade to evacuate or to seek shelter and stay off the streets, and that included Mexican police and soldiers. Anyone in the area would be considered a legitimate target until the president was secured. This could turn into a bloodbath that might play over well in the court of American public opinion, but could give the country a serious black eye on the international stage.

There had to be an alternative.

Tong turned in her chair, her eyes narrowed. "'Have you ever boiled an egg?' What do you think he means by that?"

Leroux frowned, having listened to the same update from Dawson. "I'm guessing they know they can't penetrate The Beast with anything short of a tank, but they can take its tires out, so it can't move."

"Doesn't it have run-flats?" asked Child.

"It does. But run-flats don't work if you've blown the rims off the damn car."

"Good point."

Tong gasped. "Wait a minute. You don't think they're going to light a fire under it, do you?"

"That's exactly what I think they're going to do. Boil an egg. It'll get so damn hot inside that thing, they'll be forced to evacuate or die."

Tong shivered. "What a horrible choice. Be cooked alive, or surrender to these barbarians and probably be skinned alive, or worse. We have to get them out of there before their heavy weapons arrive."

Leroux jerked his chin toward the display and the satellite footage of the motorcade. It was moving forward finally at a steady, albeit slow, pace. The problem was the map showing the computer tracking. Analysts and the AI were identifying hostiles or potential hostiles in the area. There were hundreds, and they were continuing to converge. Police and military were consolidating around the National Palace to secure the Mexican government, and the military was securing vital infrastructure, exactly as one would expect.

The president's safety, along with the Canadian prime minister's, was being left to their respective details, something that was not part of the official plan, though at the moment, he wasn't certain that was a bad thing considering the questionable loyalty of so many of those involved, and the apparent fact uniforms appeared to be a dime a dozen.

Leroux rose. "Zoom in on the motorcade a little bit more."

Tong tapped at her workstation and the magnification increased. The front loader the Delta team had commandeered pushed aside a car with ease, allowing the motorcade to slowly weave along behind it. He watched as The Beast crept through, barely clearing the car just pushed aside. He wagged a finger at the screen. "That's the problem."

"What is?"

"The Beast. It's too big. All the other vehicles can weave in and out between the debris on the road, but The Beast can't make the sharp turns, so they have to clear a wider path."

"They'll never let him out of that. That's the only thing keeping him alive."

"No, it's slowing them up. It's what's going to get them killed. Have the computer start looking for alternate routes, but take away the constraint of the size of The Beast. And forget the whole motorcade. Let's see if we can find a path out for just two or three SUVs."

"You just want to leave the rest of them behind?" Child spun in his chair. "Dude, that's ice cold."

"Our priority is the president. If we can get him out and onto Air Force One, then we just broadcast him so that the cartels know he's gone. They might just leave the rest of the motorcade behind. And remember, if two or three SUVs can make it, the rest might as well. I just don't want the computer constrained by too many parameters. Let's eliminate The Beast, and remove the constraint of the route needing to handle several dozen vehicles in rapid fashion. They've only got five-and-a-half miles to the damn airport. If we had an open road, this would all be over in less than ten minutes. Hell, if this was NASCAR, it'd be over in two."

Tong grinned. "Yeah, but they would have just ended up in the same place." She made an oval in the air. "You know, because they always go in circles."

Child gave her a disappointed look. "If you have to explain the joke, it's not a good joke."

She flipped him the bird. "It was a good joke."

Leroux agreed. "She's right. It was a good joke. Now, let's get serious. Let's see if we can find a way out of here that Washington hasn't thought of. We know from past experience they're too constrained in their thinking. All their security is designed around Air Force One, Marine One, and The Beast. It's time for some out-of-the-box thinking."

Presidential Motorcade

Mexico City, Mexico

"We can't let that happen."

Dawson gave Special Agent Carlyle a look. "No shit. But someone wants to turn The Beast into a Broil King, and we'd better be prepared for it."

"To hell with preparing for it. Just make sure it doesn't happen."

"It might not be that easy. You have to have seen what's going on here. Everything they're doing is designed to funnel us along our own escape route. That means they have something planned for us farther down the road that we don't know about. Just delaying our inevitable arrival at the airport accomplishes nothing. There is a point where they *will* stop us."

Carlyle pursed his lips as they continued rolling forward, all four Delta units fully engaged, two at the front of the column, one at the rear, and one covering the length of the motorcade on either side. Jagger lumbered past, two large bags filled with ammo slung over his shoulders as he hurried to resupply those at the front. Several of the Secret Service SUVs were loaded with weapons and supplies for just such a contingency. If the cartels thought they could wear them down and force them to run out of ammo, they were sadly mistaken.

They had enough to fight a small war.

"You have a contingency to evac The Beast, right?"

"Of course."

"Then just make sure they're ready. As soon as the first tire is taken out, that's the sign it's starting. There's going to be no time to waste."

Carlyle let out an exasperated sigh and cursed. "You're right. Son of a bitch. I chose the wrong week not to go on vacation."

Dawson laughed. "Yeah, but then you would have missed all this."

"You make that sound like it's a bad thing."

"Personally, I'm having the time of my life."

Carlyle smacked the body armor where Dawson had taken a round earlier. "You've already been shot once. How many more times before you say it's no longer a good time?"

"Probably the first one that draws blood." He held up a pair of crossed fingers. "Fingers crossed."

Carlyle laughed. "You Delta boys are a special breed."

"It's why they don't let us play with others." Dawson hopped off the running board. "Just be ready. I guarantee you, it's coming."

"We'll be ready, Sergeant Major. But hopefully you can prevent it from happening."

"I make no promises!" shouted Dawson as he sprinted ahead to rejoin the others.

Belme Residence, West Luzon Drive

Fort Liberty, North Carolina

Maggie exchanged victorious high-fives with the others as the map disappeared off the screen and the announcer issued a statement attempting to cover their asses for their stupidity. It didn't matter. The network could deal with the ramifications later. For now, all she and the others cared about was that the exact location and planned route of their loved ones were no longer telegraphed directly to the enemy.

Her phone vibrated with a message and she smiled to see it was from Clancy.

Thanks for the heads up.

She replied.

Thanks for taking care of it so quickly.

A thumbs-up appeared.

"Who was that?" asked Shirley.

"The colonel. Just thanking us for the heads up about that bullshit." She flicked her wrist at the screen.

"At least someone has his ear," said Vanessa. She pointed at Maggie. "Don't you ever quit that job."

She laughed. "I don't plan to. At least not as long as BD's in the Unit. How else am I going to keep tabs on him?"

Shirley sighed, sipping her water, carbonated via her SodaStream with a twist of lemon. "I think I prefer my ignorant bliss."

"Me too," agreed Angela. "It's bad enough just knowing what he does for a living and that every time there's something major on the news he might be involved. But to actually know that he was…" She reached out and squeezed Maggie's hand. "I don't know how you do it."

"First of all, you know what you're getting into. You were lucky you figured it out before you were in too deep with Niner, so you had the choice. And I, of course, knew before things began. I had to give it some serious thought before I decided to pursue him." She flashed a toothy smile. "But I couldn't resist those pecs and abs."

Shirley leaned in and shoulder-bumped her. "Don't forget the buns."

"Ooh, how could I?"

Everyone giggled, the tension momentarily broken before a live report from Aynslee Kai had them all focusing on the television once again.

This could be the longest day of their lives.

Presidential Motorcade

Mexico City, Mexico

"Have you witnessed any casualties yet, Aynslee?"

Aynslee shook her head. "None that I've seen, though we have a very limited vantage point. We have witnessed a lot of bodies in the streets, many of them wearing police and army uniforms, but we have no idea whether they're imposters. Chatter I've overheard indicates we shouldn't trust anyone wearing a local uniform."

"Have you heard anything on the crews of the three downed choppers?"

"No, John, I haven't heard anything. In fact, this is the first I'm hearing of it. We witnessed the three helicopters leave the National Palace when we were evacuating, and most of us had assumed the president was on board one of them. It wasn't until the motorcade was underway that we were informed he wasn't."

Bullets pinged off the vehicle and Aynslee instinctively ducked, though Roy didn't flinch.

"Get your heads down!" ordered the Secret Service driver.

Aynslee crouched, as did Roy. "John, we're going to have to let you go. We've come under fire again and are being advised to take cover."

"You stay safe, Aynslee, and get back to us when you can."

Aynslee switched off her mic, but Roy kept filming. "Make sure you turn the transmitter off."

"Already done. I'm just recording."

Aynslee made herself as comfortable as possible in the cramped quarters as heavy gunfire on either side of them responded. Their driver cursed, looking over at his partner, Agent Clarke, in the passenger seat. "Did he just say what I think he said?"

Clarke nodded. "They wanna know who's got room in case they evacuate The Beast."

"I can't believe they'd consider that."

"They must know something we don't."

Aynslee pushed up on an elbow, poking her head between the two men, and Clarke cursed.

"Please, tell me that didn't go out live."

"No, we're not transmitting. Not after the bullshit they pulled."

"You can't repeat that. You can't tell that to Atlanta. If it leaks, you could be killing the president."

"Don't worry, it doesn't leave Mexico, not until this is all over. You have my word. Have they ever taken him out of The Beast before?"

Clarke shook his head. "We've never been in a situation like this before with the president."

"But you've planned for it, haven't you?"

"Of course." Clarke tapped the door. "And all the vehicles in the motorcade are reinforced, armor plating and bullet-resistant glass, so he'd be fairly safe in anything we have."

"But is that enough?"

He frowned. "It'll have to be."

"But I thought The Beast had comms and everything the president needs to do his job?"

"It does."

A pit formed in Aynslee's stomach. "Wait a minute. What does that mean for who controls the country? Doesn't the law say that if the president is in peril and communications are lost, that the vice president takes over?"

Clarke exchanged a glance with his partner. "In theory, yes."

"And in practice?"

"We've never been in this situation before. When Air Force One went down a couple of years ago, he was presumed dead, so the vice president took over until it was discovered he was still alive and communications were reestablished. This is different."

"But is it?"

He gave her a look. "Listen, Ms. Kai, this conversation's way above my pay grade. Nobody in this motorcade will be making that decision. That'll all be back in Washington. I suggest you have one of your reporters there ask at the next press conference. For now, we need to be focusing on getting the hell out of here alive."

Aynslee gave him a smile. "You're right, of course." She retreated back to her tiny piece of real estate, her mind racing. If the president was about to leave The Beast, was there about to be a transition of power in Washington?

Garza Cartel Compound

Somewhere in the Sierra Madre Occidental Mountains, Mexico

Garza smirked at the video feed. "You have them secured?"

"Yes, sir. The entire family."

"Good. Make sure it's clear to her what happens if she doesn't cooperate."

"Trust me, sir, I'll leave no doubt."

Garza ended the call and Maria sipped on her glass of wine, something that had become a fixture in her hand since she had arrived.

"Is this going to work?"

He shrugged. "It's a long shot, but it should."

"It better. If she refuses to cooperate, I'll kill the bitch's children myself."

He regarded her. He had no doubt she would. If someone had asked him to describe her two weeks ago, he would say she was sweet and wouldn't hurt a fly, but it was as if a switch had been flipped, and he wondered what the trigger truly was. Was it outrage that her husband had been taken by the Americans? Was it that she had been drugged? Was it that the father of her children had been taken? Or was it that she feared being forced to return to the life of a stripper where she had been found years ago?

It was something he wasn't supposed to know about. The official story was that she was a waitress, but his brother had confided in him after a bottle of tequila had been put away, and it had been a shocker. They all had pieces on the side, including strippers and prostitutes, but they never married them.

The favorite was to marry the girl next door, someone who would appreciate what you had to offer and was less likely to challenge you for fear of returning to a meager existence. But you never married the whore.

"What are you looking at?" she snapped, and he flinched.

"Sorry. I was lost in thought."

She tapped her nose. "My face is up here." His head jerked up and he was slightly embarrassed to find he had been staring at her store-bought chest the entire time. He had always been attracted to her. She was a stunning woman. His own wife was gorgeous, but Maria was an entirely different level—there had never been any question as to why his brother was attracted to her, and perhaps she was indeed stunning enough to overlook her chosen vocation.

She indicated her breasts. "These belong to your brother as long as he draws breath."

He regarded her, taking a chance, the intoxicating sense of power he had while sitting in this chair getting the better of him. "And should he not?"

She eyed him, an eyebrow slowly rising before the corners of her lips curled up. "Then perhaps you and I shall have a discussion."

He smiled. "Perhaps we shall."

Vice President's Residence

Number One Observatory Circle, US Naval Observatory

Washington, D.C.

Rosalind tucked the covers around the infant with one hand, the other pressing the phone against her ear. "Yes, Madam Vice President, she just went down for her nap."

"When she wakes up, tell her Mommy misses her."

"I will, ma'am."

"Can you put Ricky on the phone?"

"He's outside playing catch with one of the agents. I can get him if you want."

"No, never mind. I have to go anyway. I assume you've heard what's happening."

"Yes, ma'am. It's terrifying."

"It is. Do you have family in Mexico City?"

"Some. No one close. Most of my family is in Guadalajara."

"Well, hopefully this violence doesn't spread. I'll need you to stay tonight, if that's okay. I don't think I'll be coming home until this is over."

"No problem, ma'am. I already told my husband not to expect me."

"Thank you, Rosalind. It's appreciated. I'll talk to you later."

The call ended and Rosalind returned to the kitchen, putting the phone in its cradle.

"Everything good?" asked Darbinger, one of the Secret Service agents assigned to the house.

She smiled weakly, troubled by what was happening in the country in which she had been born. "That was the vice president. She was just checking on the children."

"Yeah, I don't blame her." He nodded toward the television screen, the news on low. "This is insane." He gestured at drone footage from above the motorcade. "They might have to take him out of The Beast. The moment Washington loses communications with him, your boss becomes president."

Rosalind's eyes shot wide. "Really? Even if he's not dead?"

"It'll be temporary, but she'll technically be in charge until we can reestablish communications." He tapped the arm of his chair. "This household could be about to become very important, and you're about to become the presidential nanny."

Her chest swelled with pride at the thought, momentarily forgetting the reason for the promotion. She frowned. "Let's hope it doesn't come to that." She headed to the laundry room to check on a load she had in the dryer when her cellphone vibrated in her pocket. She fished it out and smiled. It was her sister, Liliana. They hadn't spoken since the Night of Reckoning, when lines all across America were jammed with loved ones around the globe calling home to see if family and friends had survived the night. It had been terrifying. She had never been at risk since she had been here, but her husband and children had ridden it out, huddled behind furniture stacked against the door.

She took the call. "Liliana, what a pleasant surprise. I can't really talk now, though, I'm at work. Is everything all right?"

"It will be if you cooperate."

Her heart leaped into her throat and she reached out, gripping the still-tumbling dryer. "Who is this?"

"I'm the man who holds the life of your entire family in his hands. I have your two sisters, three nieces, and four nephews, plus your father."

Her world closed in around her. "Are they all right?"

"I'm going to kill one of your nephews right now, just so I know I have your attention."

She felt faint then she collapsed against the wall, sliding down it. "Please, don't! You have my attention, I promise!"

"We'll see. But trust me when I say, if you don't do exactly what I tell you, everyone here is dead. And someday soon, that husband and those two children of yours will join them. Only you'll be left alive to remember that you were the one who could have saved them all."

"What do you want? What do you want from me?"

"You're at the vice president's house?"

She inhaled sharply, holding the breath for a moment. "Yes."

"And the children are there?"

She closed her eyes, terrified of where this was heading. "Yes."

"Then this is what you're going to do."

Operations Center 2, CIA Headquarters

Langley, Virginia

Leroux cursed then shot to his feet, pointing at the satellite footage covering the immediate conflict zone, scores of men rushing out of buildings toward the battle. "What the hell's going on?"

Tong shrugged. "It looks like they were in hiding."

"How many?"

"I don't know yet. The computer is still counting, over one hundred."

"It looks like at least double that."

The mission comms overhead crackled with a warning from Control. Dawson's voice cut in. "This is Bravo Zero-One. Switch the package now. I repeat, switch the package now. This could be our last chance."

"Acknowledged," replied a voice Leroux recognized as the head of the Secret Service on the scene. "Switching the package."

Leroux stepped toward the displays. "Give me a tighter angle on The Beast."

Tong manipulated the image and it zoomed in. Both front doors swung open as two agents stepped out, slamming the doors behind them as agents from other vehicles joined them to provide cover. The rear door opened and several aides scrambled out, followed by the Canadian prime minister, who reached back and helped the president out. Everyone headed to their assigned vehicle, all having been briefed earlier on what would happen if the switch was ordered, and in seconds everyone was secured inside their new rides while the driver jumped back into The Beast, continuing to advance as the area was swarmed.

"Rooftops!" warned Child, and Leroux's eyes darted to see what he was talking about.

Half a dozen men were rushing along nearby rooftops, weapons slung over their shoulders. "Are those recoilless rifles?"

Therrien confirmed it. "Looks that way. They won't penetrate The Beast, but they'll take out the tires."

"Start reviewing the footage. See if there's anything that suggests they know we did the switch. And where do we stand on that alternate route?"

Danny Packman raised a hand. "I might have something on that."

Presidential Motorcade

Mexico City, Mexico

Dawson signaled for the team to fall back and consolidate around the motorcade. Atlas hopped down from the front loader and sprinted for cover.

"Ground Team, Control, watch your rooftops. We've got half a dozen with heavy weapons, over."

Dawson didn't acknowledge the report. Instead, he issued orders to deal with it. "Charlie Team, Bravo Zero-One. Cover the rooftops, over."

"Acknowledged, Zero-One."

From the corner of his eye he caught the other Delta team redeploying to opposite sides of the streets to cover the rooftops across from them. The buildings weren't high, only four stories, but it would be difficult. Only one shot could disable The Beast then their switch would be discovered when they abandoned the vehicle. He opened fire on the portion of the intersection in his arc, eliminating three hostiles, the rest of the security teams doing the same.

"Control, Zero-One. Where the hell is that air support?"

"Inbound now, Zero-One. Keep your heads down."

The thunder of Apaches overhead filled the air, rockets launching from their weapons pods as chain guns spat over 600 rounds per minute of explosive ammunition at the enemy converging on the area.

An explosion behind him was something he couldn't ignore. He glanced over his shoulder to see The Beast had taken a hit, its front driver's side tire a twisted wreck. He cursed. Any advantage they had hoped to gain by tricking the enemy was lost, though if they were lucky, the cartels had no idea which SUV the president was in, and now that The Beast was no longer a limiting factor, they might use it to their benefit.

"Ground Team, Control. The enemy's breaking off. I repeat, the enemy is breaking off, over."

The sustained gunfire dwindled on both sides, and Dawson rose from behind his cover, thankful for the momentary reprieve, though curious as to why it had been granted. He pointed at the loader. "Atlas, get your ass back in there. Let's get moving!"

"You got it, BD." Atlas lumbered forward, back to his previous post, as Bravo Team advanced to cover him. Dawson fell back to the lead Secret Service escort, and Carlyle's window rolled down.

"Looks like you called that one, Sergeant Major."

"It made sense. But what I don't understand is why they fell back. Even if they knew we did the switch already, you'd think they'd press the advantage, so why the hell have they stopped the attack? It doesn't make any sense."

Carlyle shook his head. "I have no idea, but I'm not about to look a gift horse in the mouth. Let's take advantage of it while we can." He tapped his earpiece. "Control is reporting roadblocks the entire way, so no matter what happens, it's going to take us a long time to get to that damn airport. But my thinking is, as long as they're holding off, we should stick to the route. It's gridlock everywhere else."

Dawson wasn't as confident in that decision as Carlyle appeared to be, but didn't have a better one to offer. Control was still seeking an alternate route and so far nothing they had come up with was better than what they were on, especially if the enemy had backed off. "Let's do it your way, Special Agent, but do what we talked about. I want those SUVs shuffling like a deck of cards. If they know which one the president's in, by the time we cover the next mile, I don't want them to have a clue."

White House Situation Room

Washington, D.C.

Terri Higgins yelped as an explosion tore at the president's limousine, the feed from an overhead drone playing on a large screen in the Situation Room buried under the White House. She had to remind herself that the president was no longer inside, and she breathed a sigh of relief as the lone Secret Service agent left to drive what was now a decoy stumbled out, having survived the blast.

The Chief Justice of the United States stepped into the room. "Madam Vice President, it's time."

Everyone rose and Vice President Thomas drew a breath and held it for a moment before speaking. "Are we certain it's necessary?"

"Yes, ma'am, it is. The Twenty-Fifth Amendment to the Constitution, Section Three, states that—"

Thomas waved him off. "I know, I know. I just never thought he would transmit the declaration."

"This is procedure, ma'am, and the Constitution's been set up to address exactly this type of situation. Once the president is secure and back with proper communications, then your temporary assignment to his role will be rescinded. If we're lucky, this will all be over in an hour or two."

"If we're lucky." Thomas grunted. "I'm not sure I would phrase it the same way, Mr. Chief Justice." She regarded the sterile room, built for war. "I think a solemn occasion such as this deserves a more appropriate venue."

"The Oval Office, ma'am?"

She dismissed the suggestion. "That's not my office. That's his. And it'll remain so until this crisis is over. We'll do it in my office."

"Then I suggest we hurry, ma'am. At the moment, our country has no leader."

Vice President's Residence

Number One Observatory Circle, US Naval Observatory

Washington, D.C.

Rosalind flinched as the buzzer to the front gate sounded. The Secret Service would deal with it, but she knew who it was. She squeezed her burning eyes shut, filled with shame at what she was doing, yet she had no choice. She had spoken with her sister and she had confirmed everything. The cartel had their entire family, and they were dead if she didn't cooperate.

But she had at least saved one of the children. Ricky would survive this, but the precious little Diedre might not. She had to assume the cartels wanted the baby as a bargaining chip so they wouldn't harm her, but she knew what they were capable of. They were brutal, vicious, without any morals. They wouldn't hesitate to kill a baby if they didn't get their way.

She tied up the laundry bundle.

God, please forgive me.

The intercom buzzed. "Rosalind, did you order a dry cleaning pick-up?" It was Agent Darbinger.

"Yes, I did. Is he here already?"

"Yes. He's at the front gate."

"Let him in, please."

"You know you're supposed to tell us these things."

"I'm sorry, I forgot. I hadn't planned on needing them, but there's a stain on the missus' dress that I couldn't get out."

Darbinger said something into his radio before responding. "No problem. Just try not to let it happen again."

"I'll try, sir. Have him go to the delivery entrance."

"Already done."

She headed for the side of the house, the bundle clasped in her hand, and opened the side door as a laundry service truck pulled up and a man stepped out.

"I'm here for a pick-up."

She held out the bag and he reached for it, the sleeve of his crisp, white jacket sliding up his wrist, revealing a terrifying set of tattoos. He took the bag and stepped back into the truck, placing it in the rear before climbing back behind the wheel.

"Thank you, ma'am."

He pulled away, turning around and back toward the gate as she stared after him, tears streaming down her cheeks. She watched as he cleared the gate then she went back inside, heading for the kitchen where she retrieved a chef's knife and ran it across her wrist, the guilt too much.

She didn't deserve to live. This had been an impossible choice, to offer up the life of the most innocent, to save others equally so.

The punishment for her crime would be left up to God, not the men and women that had created a world so cruel.

Vice President's Office, The White House

Washington, D.C.

Terri Higgins gulped as the brief yet historically important ceremony concluded. Her heart hammered with the implications. The vice president was now the president, though everyone prayed it was only a temporary thing. Yet, for the first time in history, a woman was the President of the United States of America. Part of her succumbed to the moment, giving in to the pride she felt that finally someone other than a man would be given a chance to lead the free world. No matter how brief that reign, it might finally break the last glass ceiling that seemed impenetrable for so long.

The vice president, or rather, the president, faced her staff. "These are trying times, and I know you all pray with me that our president will safely make it home to resume his rightful place in the Oval Office. But until then, it's our job to make sure this country continues to function and that its enemies are given no opportunity to take advantage of the current situation."

Terri flinched as the phone in her hand vibrated. It was the new president's personal line, and it rarely rang. She didn't recognize the number, and her instructions were to send calls like this to voicemail. The phone vibrated several more times before the call ended, then a text message arrived with a photo attached. Her eyes narrowed and she tapped the message then gasped. It was a baby, a baby she recognized, with a gun pointed at her head.

"What is it?" asked President Thomas.

Terri stared at her, her eyes wide, her mouth agape, then held out the phone. Thomas took it then inhaled sharply as the phone rang once again. Terri sucked in a deep breath as Thomas stared at the phone, uncertain as to what to do.

"Clear the room!" snapped Terri. Everyone stared at her. She didn't have the authority.

Thomas pointed at the door. "Yes, everybody clear the room!"

Terri made for the door when Thomas reached out and grabbed her hand. "Not you."

The last person left and Thomas took the call, putting it on speaker as Terri closed the door.

"Hello, Madam President. Congratulations on your appointment as the first woman to ever occupy the most powerful position in the world."

Thomas put the phone on her desk then inhaled deeply through her nose and squared her shoulders as she clenched her fists. It was a move Terri recognized, one that Thomas did when about to face someone she considered hostile. "Thank you. To whom am I speaking?"

"I'm disappointed you don't recognize my voice. I know you've heard it before, though it was electronically altered, so I suppose you can be forgiven for not recognizing it."

Terri felt faint, reaching out for the back of a nearby chair as she realized it was the man that had delivered the cartels' warning during the Night of Reckoning. Thomas regarded her, her eyes questioning. "It's Juan Garza," whispered Terri.

"Your friend is right. Who else is listening in?"

Thomas paled, not at being caught, but at the realization as to whom it was she was speaking with, who had sent the photo of her baby with a gun pressed to her head. "It's only me and my aide."

"And what's her name?"

Terri's heart palpitated violently and Thomas firmly shook her head. "You don't need to know that. She's unimportant and I'm not going to give you any more power over anyone else. What is it you want?"

"You received my photo?"

"Yes." Thomas pointed at the door and held her thumb and pinky finger up to her face as if it were a phone, and mouthed the words, "Call my home."

Terri nodded and quickly left the room as the conversation continued behind her. Everyone was still huddled in the other office, wondering what was going on, when Doris, the woman who had manned the phone here for as long as Terri could remember, gasped, collapsing back in her chair, the entire room spinning to see what was the matter.

"Are you sure? What's being done? Very well, I'll inform her."

Doris ended the call and looked up, her face pale, her eyes filling with tears as her hands trembled.

"What is it?" asked someone.

Terri made eye contact. It was clear what had Doris so upset. "Rosalind, the president's nanny, attempted to kill herself a few minutes ago."

Terri's shoulders slumped. Rosalind must have helped the cartels kidnap the baby, then tried to kill herself over the guilt. She opened the door to Thomas' office and stepped inside, closing it quietly as the conversation continued, though no longer on speaker.

"I understand. Call me in thirty minutes." She ended the call and slammed the phone down on the desk, not nearly as satisfying an action with a cellphone as it was with an old-style landline.

"What did they want?"

Thomas frowned. "Are you sure you want to know?"

Presidential Motorcade

Mexico City, Mexico

"Ground Team, Control. This is to inform you that as of 1:32 PM Eastern, Vice President Thomas has been sworn in as president until the package is secure and back in communication with Washington."

Red glanced over at Dawson. "Does this change our day?"

Dawson shrugged. "I doubt it. Let's hope she's got the balls for the job." He continued to jog alongside the loader, enemy activity almost nonexistent, though the going was slow with so much debris on the road that Atlas had to clear a path through. "Margaret Thatcher did, but I hope she doesn't get too comfortable behind that chair in the Oval Office, because I intend to deliver the president I woke up to this morning back to Washington, come hell or high water."

Red jerked his chin at the road ahead. "Is this making any sense to you?"

Dawson grunted. "I'm glad I'm not the only one who's picking up on this. There's definitely something wrong. They went to all that effort to take out The Beast and then they just give up? It doesn't make any sense. They should be pressing their advantage now. Why would they hurt us along this route all this time, take out The Beast, then immediately break off?"

"The Apaches?"

Dawson dismissed the idea. "Didn't stop them before. We've killed hundreds of them and they kept coming. They're like fanatics. They had a mission, and as far as I can tell, that mission was to disable The Beast, not kill the president."

Red aimed up at a rooftop then lowered his weapon. "Okay, let's assume that was their mission, to get him out of The Beast. Why here? I was looking at the map. There's no way to get back to the National Palace or to our embassy. With The Beast out of commission, that means there's no source of secure comms except Air Force One at the airport."

Dawson's jaw dropped. "Holy shit, they never wanted him!"

Red's eyes narrowed. "What do you mean?"

"I mean, they didn't want the president. They don't give a shit if he's dead or alive as long as he's no longer the president."

"Wait a minute. Are you saying they wanted Vice President Thomas to be named president?"

"Yes."

"Why? You don't think she's crooked, do you?"

Dawson shrugged. "They're all crooked, aren't they? They're politicians. But no, I don't think she's in the pocket of the cartels."

"Then why would they do it?"

"I don't know, but I don't like it." Dawson pulled out his phone and dialed an old friend who could look into something he didn't dare put out over official comms.

Bangkok Marriott Hotel

Bangkok, Thailand

CIA Operations Officer Dylan Kane jerked back awake, his CIA-customized Tag Heuer watch sending electrical pulses into his wrist in a coded pattern, indicating he had a private communique through his secure network from a friend.

It was the middle of the night in Bangkok, but he had just been woken moments earlier with another urgent communique from Langley. The country had a new president. He didn't particularly care. One was as bad as the next. Even if they were from different parties, he had little to no faith in politicians. These days, the partisanship was disgusting. Nobody cared about what was good for the country anymore, only what was good for their party.

America was a failing democracy, and unless it got its act together soon, he wasn't sure what would happen, but he was prepared for it. He had enough money set aside that he and his girlfriend, Lee Fang, could disappear to anywhere in the world and live a comfortable life with new identities. He even had enough to bring his family with them if they wanted to come, plus a few friends like Leroux and Sherrie.

There were compounds being set up all over the world by vets who saw what was coming. Belize sounded nice, and he had friends there that had already set up a community. But for now, he would do his damnedest to save his country from itself by doing his job and doing it well, for even if Republicans and Democrats were determined to destroy the country so the other side couldn't have it, so were its enemies.

He logged into his phone and brought up the message from his old comrade-in-arms, Dawson, whom he had served with in Delta before being recruited into the CIA. He listened to the message, concern growing at its implications. If his old friend was right, the cartels had orchestrated Vice President Thomas' takeover of the presidency. It was a serious concern.

He fired a message back to his friend so he could focus on saving the legitimate president.

I'll look into it.

Unfortunately, there was nothing he could do, not from where he was. All he could do was pass on the concern to someone he trusted, and someone who could look into it. He forwarded the voicemail to his best friend, then lay back down. He had a big day ahead of him, regardless of whether a coup had just taken place back home.

Operations Center 2, CIA Headquarters

Langley, Virginia

Leroux checked his phone to see a message had arrived through Kane's secure app. Very few people in the world had access to it, and inside this operations center, only he and Tong were even aware of it.

He logged in and saw the message from Kane, then listened to Dawson's voicemail. He leaned back, gripping his temples, his eyes shut as he processed the Delta operator's theory. It was an interesting one, and it made sense to a point. If the cartels had continued attacking after The Beast was disabled, he would have dismissed the theory, but the fact they broke it off immediately suggested there was something to it.

Anyone in the know would be aware that as soon as the president lost communications, the vice president would be sworn in, but he didn't for a second believe the woman was on the cartels' payroll. Did they feel, perhaps, that she might be easier to negotiate with, that having her as president could end this reclassification of the cartels as terrorist organizations? If so, to what end?

They had backed off. If they continued to back off, then the president would reach Air Force One and would be president again. What use was there of declaring an end to the war for perhaps an hour or two? What could they possibly accomplish in such a short period of time? And even if they could force her hand, how could they do it so quickly? Even if they launched another Night of Reckoning, it would be hours before she might capitulate, and she would no longer be in power.

For the life of him, he couldn't think of what the cartels could possibly hope to gain by having her in power for an hour or two. He had no idea what they were up to, but they had to be up to something. The question was, what was that something, and what leverage could they possibly have over the new president over the old?

And more importantly, what the hell could he possibly do about it?

Vice President's Office, The White House

Washington, D.C.

"Only you and I know what's going on, understood?"

Terri's entire body trembled, paralyzed with fear. "Yes, ma'am. But shouldn't we tell someone?"

"No. The Secret Service is trying to find my baby and so far we've kept it quiet, but we both know they won't find her in time. There's only one way to save her, and that's to do what they want."

"But, ma'am, what they want, you can't do it."

"Excuse me?"

"It's not right. All the blood that's been spilled, everything, it'll have all been for nothing if you do this."

"I don't have a choice. They said they'd boil my baby alive." Thomas' eyes filled with tears, her lower lip trembling. "I can't let that happen."

"I understand that, ma'am. You're a mother and that's your baby and that's why they're using you. But you have to think of the bigger picture.

You have to tell somebody, take the decision out of your hands. Step down if necessary, let the Speaker of the House take over."

Thomas dismissed the suggestion. "No, I have to do this, it's the only way."

"And what happens when people find out what you did and why?"

"They'll understand."

"You could go to prison."

"I don't care what happens to me as long as my baby is safe. We both know this was inevitable. The cartels were never going to stop. At what point would we have ended this? Ten thousand dead? A hundred thousand? There's no way we can defend against the criminals on our own streets unless we want to turn this country into a military state and have troops on every corner. Curfews, mass arrests. This isn't Russia, this isn't China. Eventually, the president would have had to capitulate. All I'm doing is what he would have been forced to do, but sooner. When he's back in power, it'll save him face. Now, get the Chief Justice back in here and the Attorney General. I want to get this over with as quickly as possible." She aimed a finger at her. "And remember, nobody knows what's going on. That's an order from your president."

Terri gulped. "Yes, ma'am." She hurried from the room, not sure of what was the right thing to do, but certain what she was about to do was the wrong thing.

Belme Residence, West Luzon Drive

Fort Liberty, North Carolina

Maggie stared at the screen, puzzled though relieved. The latest reports from CNN were that the attack had stopped and the motorcade was slowly picking its way through the streets of Mexico City and heading for the airport. Estimates were that it would take well over an hour to cover the distance, and that assumed they didn't come under attack again.

The coverage broke away for the first time in over an hour, with a breaking news alert.

Police activity at the vice president's home.

"I wonder if she were a man, would they still be calling her vice president?" asked Vanessa.

"Probably not," said Maggie. She leaned closer to the television. "Turn it up."

Shirley increased the volume and they watched an overhead shot showing a heavy police presence around the vice president's residence and what was clearly an extensive search of the grounds taking place inside, mostly by men and women in suits that she had to assume were Secret Service.

"What do you think they're looking for?" asked Vanessa.

Maggie shrugged. "A bomb, maybe?"

Shirley disagreed. "I doubt it. They'd evacuate the grounds. This is an all-hands-on-deck search for something, and whatever it is can't be dangerous."

"We're now receiving reports from witnesses that an ambulance was seen leaving the vice president's residence less than fifteen minutes ago. A request for a comment from the White House has gone ignored, and we're looking into who was in the ambulance and where they were taken. So, to recap, all we know at this moment is that less than fifteen minutes ago an ambulance was seen leaving the vice president's property, and now there is a significant police presence and a search underway on the grounds. For what or who, we don't know at this time."

Shirley turned the volume back down. "They don't know anything."

"I wonder who it could have been?" asked Vanessa. "The president's at the White House. Could it be one of the kids?"

Shirley dismissed the idea. "No. If it were one of her kids, there's no way she'd still be at the White House. I don't care if I was in the middle of a nuclear war, if I found out one of my kids had been taken in an ambulance to a hospital, nothing would stop me from being at their side." She gestured at the screen. "And there's no way the world's first female president sneaks out of the White House."

"Her husband?"

Maggie pointed at the chyron at the bottom of the screen. "It says he's in California."

"Then it has to be a staff member or one of the Secret Service."

"But what are they searching for?" Vanessa shook her head. "If it were just something medical, why the search? Something has to have happened. Maybe somebody phoned in a threat. Whoever took the call had a heart attack."

Maggie grunted. "As good a guess as any. But what kind of a threat that isn't a bomb threat has you searching?"

Shirley frowned. "I don't know, but whatever it is, with everything going on, it can't be good."

The coverage flipped back to Mexico City and everybody fell silent, the new president's problem forgotten as they focused on their loved ones and prayed the momentary reprieve that appeared to have been granted, continued.

Vice President's Office, The White House

Washington, D.C.

"Can it be done?"

The chief justice nodded, as did the attorney general, who spoke. "Yes, Madam President, it can be done. The question is, why would you want to do it? It's political suicide. Thousands of Americans are dead and they're demanding justice. If you do this, your political career is over."

She held up her phone. "I received a private communication from Juan Garza."

The attorney general's eyebrows shot up. "Really? When?"

"Only moments after I was sworn in."

"What did he want?"

Terri, sitting in the corner, working her phone, paused, exchanging a look with the new president. Would she reveal the truth? God, she hoped so. News had already broken that something had happened at the residence, though for the moment, the press was in the dark as to what that was. It should come from the president. It shouldn't come from some leak.

"He told me that if I didn't do this, another Night of Reckoning would happen, starting this evening and repeating every night until I capitulated. I don't have a choice. America doesn't have a choice. The president made a mistake. I think we can all admit that now. We should have just taken one, not eleven of them. We overachieved, and now we're paying the price. We have to put an end to this, and there's only one way to do that."

"But Madam President, you're only going to be president for another hour, maybe two. You can't."

Thomas glared at the attorney general. "I can't? Excuse me. Am I not the president with all the power and authority that goes with the title?"

The man took a step back. "Yes, ma'am."

"Then you'll follow my orders, or I'll find someone who will."

He drew a breath, squaring his shoulders before shocking the room. "Then you have my resignation, Madam President. I cannot in good conscience do what you ask. I believe it to be a mistake and that it will go against the wishes of, if you'll forgive me, ma'am, the real president, who will be back in power before the afternoon is out, and due to the nature of what you asked, will have no way to reverse what you want to do."

Thomas bristled then forced a smile, extending a hand. "Thank you for your service. I accept your resignation."

The hand was shaken and the former attorney general left the room.

Thomas turned to Terri. "Get me Adrian Stottlemeyer."

"Yes, ma'am." Terri leaped to her feet and headed for the door.

"Are you going to fight me on this?"

The chief justice regarded Thomas. "No, ma'am. Constitutionally, you are the president and it is within your right to do this. From a constitutional standpoint, which is where my power lies, there's nothing unconstitutional about what you're doing, no matter how disagreeable or cowardly some people may find it."

"So, you think I'm a coward?"

Terri glanced over her shoulder, desperate to stay in the room, but Thomas flicked her wrist at the door.

"No, ma'am. But I think there's something else going on here that you're not telling us."

Terri closed the door, cutting off the conversation.

Just tell him the truth!

Garza Cartel Compound

Somewhere in the Sierra Madre Occidental Mountains, Mexico

"It's been thirty minutes, Madam President. Why haven't you done what you promised me?"

"It's taking longer than I thought. My attorney general refused to cooperate, and I'm trying to swear in another one as we speak."

"You're the president, Madam President, and I don't believe you. I believe you're stalling, trying to find an alternative. I see on the news that the police are at your house, and I have no doubt a manhunt is underway for my people who took your baby. I'll tell you what, I'll give you ten minutes. That's about how long it will take for the pot of water to boil."

"No, please!"

Garza smirked at Maria, who sat with a half-empty glass of chardonnay on the couch in her husband's office. "Ten minutes, Madam President, but if you require more time, perhaps I can provide that to you as well. I can kill your former boss."

He ended the call and Maria rose, slinking seductively toward him. "I had no idea you were so vicious."

He smiled. "The only reason I haven't been in charge is because I was born second."

"Then perhaps it's your time to shine."

"Perhaps it is." He picked up the phone and hit one of the speed dials. It was answered immediately.

"Yes, sir?"

"There might be a delay. Buy us some time."

"Yes, sir. Consider it done."

He hung up the phone and faced Maria.

"If you kill him, they'll never stop hunting for you."

He smiled. "They have to find me first."

Garza Cartel Compound

Copper Canyon, Mexico

Sherrie lay prone on the ground, Rivas beside her. They had parked several miles away and hiked it in with guidance from Langley, Raul's final switch taking him along a dirt road and into a hidden entranceway leading into the mountainside. This was obviously Salvador Garza's bunker, the secret lair from which he claimed he could run his empire and hold out against any opponent. But he was now in prison and his brother was using it to wage a war that had to be stopped.

"So, what do you think?" asked Rivas.

"I think there's no doubt this is it."

"How deep do you think it goes?"

She shrugged. "I don't know, and there's no way to really know without going in there."

Rivas' eyebrows shot up as he rolled on his side to stare at her. "Please tell me you're not thinking of going in there."

She chuckled. "Oh, I'm thinking about it, but I'm not going to. I'm not a fool. There's no way to sneak in. We found him, we know where he is, now let's see if we can figure out where his comms relays are. If we can take those out, we shut down his ability to give orders."

"But won't he just leave?"

She pointed at the entrance and the mountain it sat at the bottom of. "If we have that mountain come down on top of him, I don't think he's going to be going anywhere. Now, let's find those relays."

Presidential Motorcade

Mexico City, Mexico

"Bravo Zero-One, Control. We have enemy activity converging on your area, over."

Dawson cursed, as did several of the others who had heard the update. "Copy that, Control. Can you be more specific, over."

"It appears that the entire force that's been shadowing you is now heading directly for you from all directions. Whatever reprieve you had appears to be about to end."

"Copy that, Control. Have those gunships soften them up again. The fewer that reach us, the fewer we have to deal with."

"Roger that, Zero-One, gunships are en route. Control, out."

Dawson activated his comms. "This is Bravo Zero-One. Be advised, a large number of hostiles are inbound. It looks like we're going to be fighting our way out of this after all. Bravo Team, cover the loader. We need to keep advancing even if it is slow. Charlie Team, cover the rear. Alpha and Foxtrot, secure intersections as we pass through them and watch the rooftops. Let's do this by the numbers and we'll get through it. Zero-One, out."

The entire time he had been talking, Atlas had continued forward, shoving aside yet another car as the motorcade inched forward. They had covered two miles. There were five to go, though he had received word that the two Canadian teams had arrived at the airport and commandeered a piece of their own equipment and were clearing a path from the opposite direction, and for the moment, hadn't come under attack.

"Bravo Zero-One, Control, be advised the Mexicans are finally taking down the cellular network. That should hopefully hamper the enemy's ability to communicate when they get it done, over."

"Copy that, Control. Thank the Mexicans for finally doing the right thing that they had already agreed to, over."

Clancy's voice cut in. "Zero-One, Control Actual. I'll pass on your thanks. Cleaned up, of course."

Dawson grinned at Red. "Of course, sir."

"One of these days that mouth of yours is going to get you in trouble," said Red.

Dawson shrugged as he continued to jog forward. "That's what colonels are for. They're filters for their NCOs."

"You better hope Clancy never retires."

"I don't care if he retires, as long as he retires after me."

Gunfire filled the air behind them and Dawson sighed. "I knew it was too good to be true."

Director Morrison's Office, CIA Headquarters

Langley, Virginia

Leroux sat in front of his boss' desk as National Clandestine Service Chief Leif Morrison mulled over Dawson's theory. "If you had come in here ten minutes ago, I would've dismissed it, but there's something you're not aware of that I was just made aware of a couple of minutes ago."

"What's that?"

"There's an unconfirmed report that our new president's nanny just tried to kill herself, and that the baby she was responsible for, the president's infant daughter, is missing."

Leroux's jaw dropped. "Holy shit! That kind of changes everything, doesn't it?"

"What do you mean?"

Leroux was fully aware his boss wasn't that naïve, but was instead more interested in hearing whatever his analyst's famous gut was telling him. "If the nanny tried to kill herself, she had to have a reason, and it had to be something spur of the moment. If you've been thinking about killing yourself for a long time, you typically don't do it at work. You do it in the privacy of your own home."

"Go on."

"So, something happened at the residence, and if the baby's missing, it has to have something to do with her."

"Do you think she killed the baby?"

"No, they would've found her by now if that were the case, and these people pass psych evals. I don't think we're dealing with an unstable woman here. I think we're dealing with a woman overcome with guilt. That baby's gone. She's not on the property. I'm going to take a wild guess, but I bet you that nanny is Mexican, has family back in Mexico, and that the cartels got to them. She got that baby out of the house somehow and it's being used as leverage against our new president."

Morrison collapsed back in his chair, his head slowly shaking. "Holy shit, Chris. If there was ever a time I wanted your gut to be wrong, this is it."

"You and me both, sir. But what do we do? If the president has been compromised, is there anything that can be legally done?"

Morrison's finger rapidly tapped on the arm of his chair. "I'm not sure. Certainly nothing that could be done quickly. I'm going to have to run this up to the director, but I'm going to need proof. If I go to her with this and then you tell me the nanny is from Norway, we're both going to be looking for jobs on Monday." He pointed at the door. "Go get me the proof."

"Satellite coverage of the vice president's residence could be helpful."

"You've got it. I'll send the authorization through now. We'll sort out the jurisdictional nonsense later."

"Yes, sir." Leroux left Morrison's office, his heart hammering. Dawson's theory had been just that, a theory. Why had the cartels been hell-bent on getting the president out of The Beast? Forcing the transition of power had been an interesting idea, though it was just one of many possible motives. But if the baby of the newly sworn-in president had been kidnapped by the cartels, it changed everything. They now had leverage over her, but to what end?

They had backed off, stopping their attack on the motorcade. Why? If they were willing to let the president survive and reach the airport, he would be president again as soon as he boarded Air Force One. Whatever they were hoping to get President Thomas to do had to be something short-term, something irreversible. She could call an end to the reclassification of the drug lords as terrorists, but the moment she was back in her old position, that could be reinstated. What was it that a president could do that couldn't be undone that the cartels would want?

He boarded the elevator and his eyes shot wide as he realized exactly what was going on. "Oh, my God! It all makes sense!"

Someone on the elevator he didn't recognize glanced at him. "What makes sense?"

"Everything."

Presidential Motorcade

Mexico City, Mexico

Atlas crouched as low as he could go as bullets pinged off the metal skin of the loader. Spare body armor had been brought up from the Secret Service vehicles and was draped over the doors, seats, and every other surface he could hook them on to. He was probably safe in here if it weren't for the fact *he* was now the primary target, not the president.

From the updates he was hearing over the comms, it appeared their enemy had no idea which vehicle the president had been moved into, which meant he was the focus. If they could take him out, then they could bring the entire motorcade to a grinding halt, then simply focus on taking each SUV out individually.

Spock stumbled and Atlas caught his breath. If there was one brother who had to survive this, it was Spock. He had lost his wife recently and it would leave his children orphaned if he were to die here today. Niner raced to Spock's side and helped him up. Spock checked himself over then gave a thumbs-up to Niner before turning and delivering one to

Atlas. He patted his body armor, kissed two fingers, then held them up to Heaven before resuming the advance.

Atlas lowered the blade, slamming into a pickup truck, its tires intentionally flattened. He couldn't wait until they met up with the Canadians who were in a faster vehicle. His was on tracks, the Canadians were on wheels, so they were closing the gap far faster than he was. Thanks to them, what was going to be over an hour could be less than half of that.

Assuming they survived.

Presidential Motorcade

Mexico City, Mexico

Aynslee's pulse pounded as the gunfire's intensity continued to increase. Apache gunships hammered the ground on adjacent streets in an attempt to thin out the numbers the Special Forces teams on the ground would be forced to deal with, but too many were clearly making it through. Atlanta was in her ear wanting her to go live, but she refused. Everyone inside was taking cover. Some were screaming, others crying while she battled her own panic attack.

An explosion to their left had Clarke cursing.

"What was that?" asked Roy.

"Some sort of RPG just took out one of the SUVs."

"Was it the president's?" Aynslee managed to ask.

"No. It looks like just staffers."

Just staffers. She was certain he didn't mean that their lives were unimportant, but the qualifier just rubbed her the wrong way. She hadn't wanted her death broadcast to the world, but there was more going on here beyond just herself and her cameraman. There were well over a hundred lives that hung in the balance. She was a journalist. It was her job to document history, and what was taking place on the other side of the door she crouched against was definitely history, and those fighting and dying had a right to have their story told.

She tapped Roy's leg and he looked at her. "You good?"

"As good as can be expected. You're ready to do this?"

She gave a curt nod. "Let's do it." She activated her mic. "Chuck, it's Aynslee. We're ready to go live. Just make sure we're on that delay so we can filter out anything critical."

"You got it, Aynslee. Just tell me when you're ready."

She gave a thumbs-up to Roy who returned it, his camera already propped on his shoulder. "We're ready."

"All right. We're live in five, four, three, two, one, you're on."

Aynslee stared at the camera, the lights indicating it was recording and transmitting like switches, her emotions set aside, her fears forgotten as she became the professional that she was.

"This is Aynslee Kai reporting live from Mexico City where we are once again under heavy fire, the cartels determined to either capture or kill the President of the United States. Just moments ago—"

"Oh, shit! Everyone down!" cried Clarke. "Front—"

Roy panned the camera as Aynslee turned her head and spotted the trail of something streaking toward them.

"It's gonna hurt!" shouted Roy as Aynslee ducked, her own worst fears about to be realized—she was about to become a participant in the story rather than its documenter.

"Goodbye—" Her final words were cut off as a warhead slammed into the hood of their car, flipping it onto its side, a searing pain tearing at her as her world went black.

Belme Residence, West Luzon Drive

Fort Liberty, North Carolina

Maggie's hand darted to her chest. "Oh, my God!"

Everyone fell silent as Shirley cranked up the volume as the anchor shouted. "Aynslee, are you all right? Can you hear me?"

The screen was split with the anchor on the left, the live feed from Mexico City on the right.

"Aynslee, can you hear me?" The anchor pressed a finger against his ear. "You'll have to forgive us, folks. We're on a delay with Mexico City. It's very confusing." He pointed to someone off-screen. "No, don't go to commercial. She would want this documented."

Somebody screamed and Maggie wasn't certain for a moment whether it had come from Shirley's living room, the CNN studio, or the Mexico City feed. She tilted her head slightly in an effort to hear better. There was whimpering and crying. Somebody groaned loudly, then the camera, lying on its side, catching nothing but the floor mat, swung.

"Aynslee, are you all right?"

It was a different voice. It wasn't the anchor. It had to be somebody in the car with her. The camera swung unaimed as if whoever was holding it was simply moving it out of the way. A collective gasp escaped from the room at the sight of a man, his head pressed against a window, his neck bent at an unnatural angle, his entire body pressing down on a snapped spine.

"Aynslee, can you hear me?"

There was a groan, loud, as if it were mic'd.

"Aynslee!"

"What happened?"

Vanessa cried out, as did several of the others, at Aynslee's voice. The feed cut away, the screen replaced with the anchor and his cohost.

"We're going to go to a commercial break now while we sort things out. But for those of you at home, we have confirmed that Aynslee Kai and her cameraman Neville Roy are alive. We'll be back in a moment."

Maggie collapsed back on the couch as Shirley muted the television. "I don't know how much more of this I can take."

"Do you want me to turn it off?" asked Shirley.

"Hell, no. As long as BD and the others are out there risking their lives, the least we can do is watch."

Vanessa rose. "I don't know about you girls, but I need a drink."

Shirley seconded the motion and headed for the kitchen with Vanessa. "I think we all deserve margaritas."

Everyone rose, nervous laughter and giggles escaping, the tension of the past hour incredibly high. Maggie headed for the bathroom and closed the door, sending a text message to the colonel's private number, just a question mark. Her phone vibrated a moment later with a reply.

4

Her eyes narrowed. What did it mean? Then she smiled. Four miles. That had to be what it meant. Four miles. They were closer than what CNN had been reporting.

Maybe there was still hope.

Presidential Motorcade

Mexico City, Mexico

Dawson squeezed the trigger, his weapon on full auto as he sprinted across the next intersection, providing suppression fire as the others positioned themselves to secure the area. They had lost two SUVs so far. Lives had been lost, not from the explosions themselves, but from the aftermath. The survivors were being redistributed now, but soon all the vehicles would be beyond capacity. The Secret Service would be the first to take to the streets, but if they didn't change the equation soon, civilians would be running defenseless in the open.

They had less than four miles to go to meet up with the Canadians. Atlas' loader was taking a beating, but it kept rolling forward like the tank it was, inexorably clearing a path as long as someone was behind the controls, though it would be the Canadians and their much faster-wheeled loader that would be narrowing the distance in any appreciable amount.

"Bravo Zero-One, Control, come in, over."

"Go ahead, Control."

"Our friends at Langley have a suggestion. The route you're on takes a hard turn up ahead. They think they can cut about a mile off if you're willing to take a chance."

A mile. It would take that four number down to three, but more importantly, it might get them out of the gauntlet they found themselves stuck in. "I'm all ears."

"Up ahead, there's a parking garage on your left. It has an exit on the opposite street, then it's a clear shot along a road that's been closed for construction. That'll take you about a mile and then you'll intersect again with the original route. There's just one problem."

"What's that?"

"You have to leave the loader behind."

Dawson eyed the monster that, for the moment, was their only hope. "If we do this, how long do we have to hold out before the Canadians reach us?"

"Approximately fifteen minutes."

He cursed. Fifteen minutes stuck surrounded by countless hostiles might as well be fifteen hours, but fifteen minutes was a hell of a lot shorter than the over half-hour they were currently looking at. They had already lost two vehicles in just the past few minutes. How many more would they lose in the next thirty to forty before they met up with the Canadians?

"What are you thinking?" asked Red.

"I'm thinking if we've got a clear shot, we can get ahead of the main force. They're all repositioning to engage us here. If we can get a mile ahead unexpectedly, they're gonna have to reposition their heavy weapons, and the Apaches should keep them on foot. We'll have to hold for fifteen minutes, but we might just be able to do it."

"Sounds good to me."

Dawson sent several bursts down the street toward a cluster of the enemy. "Control, Zero-One. We're gonna do it. That route better be clear, over."

"It is, Zero-One. We've reconfirmed ourselves with satellite and drone. The entire road has been closed off for construction, so it was never part of the security operation."

"If we end up with a repeat of Speed where there's an entire section of the road that's completely missing, I'm going to be very upset."

Clancy came on the comms. "Zero-One, Control Actual. There is a section that is out, but it's beyond where you're heading. We're confident that the portion you need is clear. The only question that we can't confirm is whether you can pass through the parking garage to the other side. Langley believes you can, but it's the only thing we can't confirm, over."

Dawson bit his lip, thinking. "Copy that, Control. We're gonna send someone through. Zero-One, out." He spotted the parking garage ahead and rushed back to the lead SUV.

Carlyle lowered his window. "I hope you've got a plan, Sergeant Major, because this isn't looking good."

"I've got a plan, if it works. If it doesn't, direct all complaints to Langley."

Carlyle chuckled. "What is it?"

Dawson pointed ahead. "You see that parking garage?"

"Yeah."

"Langley says if we can get through it to the other side, it's a straight shot for one mile to rejoin this route. The road's closed for construction. Control has confirmed it's clear. We just don't know if we can get through the parking garage. We should be able to, but we need someone to confirm it."

"Consider it done."

Dawson hopped off the running board and the window rolled up as the SUV sped away, deking around the loader then cutting into the parking garage. Dawson sprinted ahead and climbed up on the loader. "As soon as we get the all-clear, we're gonna be going through that parking garage."

Atlas glanced at him. "Sounds like fun. I'm liable to take the building down on top of me, though."

"Not that much fun. When we give the signal, can you set this thing so it'll just keep driving forward?"

"Not a problem." He gestured ahead. "It's gonna go straight into that building, though."

"Doesn't matter. Even if it buys us a few minutes of them thinking we're still moving on this route, it'll have done its job. As soon as you reach that parking garage, set it and forget it."

"You got it, BD."

Dawson hopped down and Carlyle's voice was relayed through his comms.

"This is Hotel Team Leader. We've made it through to the other side. It's clear. When you enter, take your immediate left, go for about a hundred feet, then take a right and follow the exit signs, over."

"Copy that, Hotel Leader. We're coming to you now. As soon as the first vehicle reaches you, proceed. I don't want a bottleneck inside the parking garage, over."

"Copy that, Bravo Leader. We'll be ready."

Dawson sprinted toward the parking garage. "Control, put me on all comms, over."

"You're on, Zero-One."

"Copy that, Control. This is Bravo Zero-One to all ground assets. Proceed immediately into the parking garage. Take your first left, go about one hundred feet, take a right, then follow the signs to the exit. When you come out onto the opposite street, go right, then proceed at best speed. Ground Team, hitch a ride or you'll be left behind. But even if you are, it's only a mile." He pointed at the first SUV, waving his arm. "Let's go! Let's go! Let's go! This only works while they don't know we're doing it."

Four Delta members including Red hopped on the running boards and the driver hammered on the gas, racing towards Dawson's position then banking hard before disappearing into the black maw that was the garage entrance.

"Hotel Leader, Bravo Zero-One. First vehicle's on its way, over."

"Copy that, Zero-One. We're ready to go, over."

The next SUV followed as the security bubble collapsed in on the garage, Delta and Secret Service hopping aboard each SUV as it lined up to enter. The Apaches hammered the area, including the rooftops, as a rhythm was found.

Dawson hopped on the last vehicle with Niner, Atlas, and Spock. He breathed a sigh of relief as they cleared the entrance, gunfire replaced with the chirping of tires in the concrete echo chamber. "Control, Zero-One, last vehicle is clear of the street. Have the Apaches light it up. I want them wondering where the hell we went for as long as possible."

"Copy that, Zero-One. Lighting it up."

Dawson held on as they made the sharp left, the driver gunning it as the taillights of the next SUV disappeared to the right. This was going exactly according to plan, which had him nervous. Then again, Langley was good at what they did, damn good, and he had a feeling it was Leroux's team that might have just saved their bacon. He just wondered what was happening on the home front.

Had they discovered there was something to his theory?

Operations Center 2, CIA Headquarters

Langley, Virginia

Danny Packman pointed at the display. "Looks like they're using our little route."

Child spun in his chair. "Don't call it 'our' until we know it worked. Right now, if this goes south, it's all *your* fault."

Packman flipped Child the bird. Leroux chuckled as he watched the satellite footage of the motorcade now barreling down the closed road unopposed, the Apaches still tearing up the entire area the president and the others had been trapped in only moments ago.

"ETA on the Canadians?"

Tong checked her station. "Thirteen minutes. They're making good time, but the motorcade's gonna be at the next security barrier in less than two minutes. Let's hope they can hold out." Her console beeped. "I've got that footage."

Leroux snapped his fingers, pointing at the main display. "Let's see it."

Tong brought up the archival satellite footage Morrison had given them permission to look at. CIA wasn't supposed to operate on American soil, and that included looking at domestic satellite footage of the vice president's residence without authorization. "Okay, back it up to the 9-1-1 call."

Tong worked her station and the image updated.

"All right, now let's just back it up and see what happens."

"How far?" asked Tong as the footage started to reverse.

"I don't think we're going to have to go back much beyond when Thomas was sworn in if our theory's right." He pointed as a cargo van left through the front gate. "What is that?"

Tong isolated the van, the angle of the satellite giving them a decent shot of the side. "Capital Laundry."

Leroux turned. "Randy, run a check on that. See what we know about them. Sonya, let's see where he was."

She tracked the van back to the side of the residence where an exchange was made with a woman.

"Play it forward."

They watched it in the proper sequence.

"Isolate on the bag she handed over."

Tong zoomed in. "Looks like a laundry bag. Dry cleaning, maybe?"

"Probably, but something tells me there was something tucked in with their delicates. Get a shot of the woman. Let's confirm it's the nanny, and isolate the driver."

Tong worked her magic and moments later a file photo of Rosalind Perez appeared.

"That's her. And the other guy?"

"Still searching."

"Let's assume the baby's in that bag. Let's follow that truck. See where it went. Watch for any blind spots where they might have done a handover. As long as that baby is in their hands, the President of the United States is under their control."

Vice President's Office, The White House

Washington, D.C.

President Thomas pushed back from her desk and stood. "Is that it?"

The chief justice nodded. "Yes, Madam President. It's now official."

"And there's no undoing this?"

"No, Madam President, what you've done is irreversible unless you're impeached. Think of it as double jeopardy. They can't be charged with the same crime twice, and you've just pardoned them for all their previous crimes, known and unknown."

Adrian Stottlemeyer, the new attorney general, sworn in only minutes ago, stepped forward. "Madam President, it's not too late. Nobody outside this room knows what just happened. We can still destroy those papers."

Thomas vehemently shook her head. "No. I've decided upon a course of action and I'm determined to see it through." She handed the sheaf of pardons to him. "See that these are executed immediately. No delays. I want every one of them on an airplane and heading to Mexico in less than half an hour."

Stottlemeyer's eyes widened. "I don't even know if that's possible, ma'am."

"Make it happen. That's an order."

"I'll see what I can do." Stottlemeyer rushed from the room and Thomas flicked her wrist at the door. "Everybody out. I need a minute." She pointed at Terri. "Except you."

Terri gulped. She had been a fly on the wall for most of the proceedings and was convinced she was the only one besides the president who knew exactly what was going on. News had just broken that something was happening at the president's residence, but no one in the press had figured out what that something was. And now that the pardons had been issued, it didn't matter. As soon as Stottlemeyer executed the order, there was no turning back. Even if the former president was sworn back in, there was nothing he could do about it.

They were now innocent men.

The entire situation disgusted her, and the more she thought about it, the less respect she had for her boss. The woman was acting as a mother, not a president, and was setting back the women's rights movement by decades. In the aftermath of this, which would dominate the press for the coming weeks and months, the Neanderthals of society would claim she did what she did because she was a woman and weak, that a man never would have chosen family over country. Thousands were dead because of these drug lords just in the past week. That didn't include the hundreds of thousands, if not millions of lives lost and destroyed by the poison they peddled. Yes, the death of one baby was a horrible thing to contemplate, and if Thomas were any other woman, the choice would be clear. But as president, you had to put these things aside and look at the greater good of the nation.

When this was over, she would have no choice but to resign her position, then when questioned by Congress during the inevitable impeachment hearings, tell the truth about what she knew and when, ending her career before it had really begun. It wasn't fair. Thomas had been selfish, thinking only of herself and her family rather than the consequences of the rash act demanded of her.

The room emptied and Terri closed the door. Thomas said nothing for a moment, instead dropping into her chair and closing her eyes as she pinched the bridge of her nose. She let out a heavy sigh then rose and rounded the desk, taking Terri's hands, staring directly into her eyes. "When they question you, which they will, you tell them the truth. Everything, including the fact that I ordered you to remain silent about what was happening for as long as I was president."

Terri gulped. "Ma'am, you could be president for the rest of the term. The cartels are attacking the motorcade again."

Thomas pointed at one of the two couches in the room. Terri sat then Thomas positioned herself on the opposite couch. "I'm aware of that, which is why I was trying to get things done so quickly. It's the only way to save the president's life."

"What do you mean?"

"In my last conversation, it was clear that Garza didn't believe I could get the pardon in place before the president made it to the airport and resumed command. It's obvious to me that the new attack is aimed at either killing the president, which will give me much more time to get the job done, or to at least delay him long enough for me to get it done. We need to get those eleven drug lords in the air as quickly as possible so that the cartels call off their attack. Should I fail, the president is most likely dead." She sighed. "I don't think you'll have to worry about keeping this secret for very long. I'll be impeached by the end of the week. And to be perfectly frank, my intention is to resign the moment this crisis is over." She retrieved her cellphone from the desk and returned to her perch on the couch. "I want you to be witness to this call. Remember every detail. This is something the history books have to get right."

Terri held up her phone. "Perhaps I should record it?"

Thomas agreed. "Actually, do that. Otherwise, it'll be your word against the lies that will be propagated on the Internet. When this is over, put that online so everyone knows why I did what I did. It's critical that the country knows that what I did was not just the desperate act of a mother attempting to save her baby by abusing her temporary power, but that it was also the act of a president sparing her country from a terrible mistake."

"Do you think the president was wrong in arresting the cartel leaders?"

"In hindsight, yes, though at the time I supported the idea. I don't think it occurred to anybody what the response would be. The cartels were threatening indefinite repeats of the Night of Reckoning until we capitulate, and eventually this country will be forced to fall on its sword."

"But there has to be a solution."

Thomas sighed. "There has to be, but what that is, I don't know. Tighter borders, kill their foot soldiers, dry up their markets. That's all I can think of. Perhaps target one cartel at a time. All I know for sure right now is that going after all twelve of the major cartels at once just made a common enemy, and that was a mistake that I have to save our country from while I can, because you know as well as I do that the president will refuse to capitulate until it's too late, and tens of thousands more innocent Americans lie dead on the streets."

Presidential Motorcade

Mexico City, Mexico

Dawson squinted as they emerged from the parking garage and into the sunlight. The driver made a sharp right turn then floored it, sending them barreling down the empty road. The chaos continued behind them as the Apaches pounded the area, providing not only a screen for their escape, but reducing the numbers that would be sent after them. So far, Langley's plan was working perfectly, and within a couple of minutes would deliver them into another dead-end where they would be at the mercy of their pursuers who wouldn't be fooled for long.

Dawson's comms squawked. "Bravo Zero-One, Bravo Zero-Two. We've reached the barrier. We've encountered no resistance so far, over."

Dawson acknowledged the report. "Copy that, Zero-Two. Spread out, secure the area for prolonged assault, over."

"Copy that, Zero-One. Securing the area. Zero-Two, out."

There was a loud crash to their right and everyone's head spun when Atlas grinned. "I think that's my loader reaching the end of the line."

Niner made the sign of the cross. "She served us well. May she rest in peace."

Atlas grunted. "Did you see that thing? It's more like rust in peace."

Niner flashed a rock salute, his eyes maniacal, his tongue sticking out. "Megadeth, yeah!"

Spock cocked an eyebrow. "There's no way you listen to Megadeth."

"What? Asians can't listen to heavy metal?"

Atlas eyed his friend. "Oh, you can listen to heavy metal. I'm stunned Babymetal hasn't made your playlist in your car yet."

Spock gave Atlas a look. "Hey, don't be knocking Babymetal. If they're good enough for Kiss, they're good enough for me in my books."

Atlas stared at Spock, stunned. "Now, how the hell do *you* know about Babymetal?"

"I have kids. What's your excuse?"

Niner grinned. "He's got you there."

Dawson pointed ahead, ending the tangent. "Looks like we've reached the end of the road." Several dozen SUVs were stopped, all hugging the walls of the buildings lining the street. Dawson leaned down and tapped on the driver's window. It rolled down several inches. "Take us right to the front."

"You got it."

The driver blasted past the other vehicles before bringing them to a rapid halt. Dawson and the others hopped off the running boards then he quickly assessed the situation. He had four full Delta units, 48 men at his command, heavily armed and well-provisioned. They could hold out, though not indefinitely and not without casualties. He just prayed none were fatal.

Red waved and Dawson joined him. He eyed the barrier made of three rows of heavy concrete slabs bolted into the road. He beckoned Atlas, who jogged over. "Do you think we can move these?"

Atlas slung his weapon and grabbed one of the barriers with both hands and pulled. It rocked slightly. "We could probably drag the barriers out of the way if they weren't bolted to the ground. You have to cut the bolts off at the top and lift these things off with a crane, or somehow cut the bolts underneath so that we can drag them out of the way. If we had the loader, it'd be no problem. Just get the teeth under them and lift them up and move them."

Niner held up his phone. "There's a hardware store just a couple of hundred yards from here." He grinned. "Google's your friend in Mexico too."

"Good to see the Mexicans didn't bring down the cellular network like they promised." Dawson pointed at Niner. "Take half a dozen men from Charlie Team, get to that hardware store and get us equipment that can cut through these bolts. And don't forget some jacks."

"You got it," said Niner, turning to leave when Atlas stopped him.

"And get three of everything if you can. I want to be working on all three of these at once."

"You got it, big man, but I expect that by the time I'm back you'll have single-handedly lifted each of these out of the way."

"Believe you me, I'll have tried."

Dawson double-checked Red's deployments, satisfied with their defensive positions. His comms squawked.

"Zero-One, Control. It looks like the enemy's figured out what's going on. You have hostiles headed your way. ETA less than five minutes, over."

"Copy that, Control, we'll be ready. ETA on the Canadians?"

"Nine minutes out."

"Copy that, Control. Status on our air cover?"

"All four Apaches are returning to base to refuel and re-arm. I'm afraid you're on your own. They won't be at your position before the Canadians."

Dawson rolled his eyes at Red. "I suppose the Mexicans aren't willing to contribute?"

Clancy came on the line. "Zero-One, Control Actual. The Mexican president has ordered all federal, state, and municipal authorities to stand down in the conflict zone. Nobody knows who's on the right side of things here, and I'd rather not risk putting a chopper overhead with a gunner who's got a family being held by the cartels. God knows there's enough insanity going on back here. I can only imagine what's going on there."

Dawson paused. "Control, is there something we should know about?"

"Negative, Zero-One, just focus on the mission at hand. It's critical you save the president and get him back to Air Force One. Failure is not an option."

"Understood, sir. We'll get it done. Just get those Apaches back here as quickly as possible."

"Will do, Zero-One. Control Actual, out."

Red peered down the street in the direction the hostiles were approaching from. "What do you think that was all about?"

Dawson shrugged. "I don't know, but something must be going on back home, and I have a funny feeling it has to do with my theory." He pointed at Mickey. "Does your phone have Internet?"

Mickey fished it from one of his pockets. "Yeah, I'm connected."

"Check the news."

Mickey stared at him. "What?"

"Just check the news. Let me know if there's something happening we need to know about."

"You got it, but I'm sending the colonel the bill for my roaming charges."

"What do you think's going on?" asked Red.

Dawson shrugged. "I'm not sure, but it's not like the colonel to say something like that. I don't think he wanted it going out over comms during a mission, but he knew we'd check it out."

Mickey whistled, and they both turned toward him.

"What's up?"

Mickey held up his phone. "You're not going to believe this shit, but our new president just issued pardons for all eleven drug lords that we arrested the other day."

"Are you kidding me?" Dawson rubbed his shoulder, still slightly tender from where he had taken a round. A few inches higher and he would have been dead. "Why the hell is she doing that?"

"No idea. It's just a breaking news headline, says more details to follow. This is happening as we speak."

Red spat. "As we die."

Gunfire rattled at the far end of the motorcade and Dawson cursed. "Well, whatever's happening, news obviously hasn't reached our friends, otherwise they might not be so hell-bent on killing us."

"Maybe we should let them know," suggested Mickey sarcastically.

Atlas looked up from his examination of the barriers. "I'd like to volunteer Niner for that mission."

"He's already on a mission. You'd better pray he succeeds. If the cartels find out about the Canadians, taking out a wheeled vehicle is going to be a hell of a lot easier than taking out that tracked behemoth you were driving."

Jagger jogged up, holding two jacks commandeered from the SUVs. "Will these do?"

Atlas shrugged. "No idea. Let's find out."

Dawson left the big man to his work and pointed at the intersection. "Hold this position. If we lose it, we're screwed."

Red nodded. "You got it, BD. We'll hold it or die trying."

Dawson headed to the rear of the motorcade at a sprint, his mind racing as more of the puzzle pieces fell into place. His theory was that the cartels were trying to force a transition of power, and now he knew why. Presidential pardons were irreversible, and the vice president at the moment had all the power of the presidency. If she had signed the pardons already, which the news report suggested she had, then it was a fait accompli. The drug lords would be freed, all the hard work by America's Special Forces for naught, all the lives lost here today wasted, the thousands of souls massacred on the Night of Reckoning needless losses.

She had to know that what she was doing wouldn't go over well, and he had to wonder why she was doing it. He had followed the woman enough to know she was one tough cookie, and no one who knew her would call her a coward. He had to think she was being forced into this. The question was, who held sway over her? A terrified Washington regretting their actions, or the cartels threatening further retaliation? Whatever was going on, he couldn't help but wonder whether he and his men were now considered pawns that could be sacrificed for some perceived greater good.

The very notion pissed him off and made him all the more determined to get the job done and the president back in power.

Operations Center 2, CIA Headquarters

Langley, Virginia

"Control, Skylark. Tap is in place. Can you confirm it's functional, over?"

Leroux glanced over at Tong who tapped at her station then gave a thumbs-up. "Skylark, Control Actual. We've confirmed the tap is in place and functional. Recommend you take cover at a safe distance, over."

"Repositioning now, Control. Skylark, out."

Sherrie and the Mexican asset scurried away from the hidden communications relay they had located. He glanced back at Packman. "Make sure wherever they hole up is far enough away."

"Will do, boss."

Marc Therrien shouted in triumph from the back of the room and pointed at the main display, satellite footage appearing. "I found where they went." Footage played showing the laundry truck pulling into a warehouse location. "It's in Arlington. About fifteen minutes from the VP's residence."

"Get that location to Echo Team and notify the locals."

"Relaying now," said Tong as she repositioned her mic.

"Echo Team ETA?"

"They're reporting less than ten minutes."

"As soon as they arrive, tell them they're a go. Don't wait for the locals. And tell them it's shoot to kill. The only objective is the safe retrieval of the baby."

"Copy that."

Child raised a hand as if he were still in high school. "The baby story just broke. Apparently, a source at the hospital they took the nanny to is claiming the woman said she had no choice, that the cartels had taken her entire family hostage in Mexico."

Packman grunted. "Well, that has to set a record for the shortest time from swearing-in to lame-duck status."

Leroux had to agree. News was just breaking that the eleven cartel leaders in custody had been pardoned and now the nation knew why. It wasn't to end the crisis, which might have been forgivable, it was to save the life of one child, an impossible equation to balance, though the pundits would try.

America needed its president back without any encumbrances.

"ETA on the Canadians?"

"Five minutes," replied Tong. "But the hostiles have reached the motorcade. And here's more good news."

Leroux groaned. "What's that?"

"The cartels have engaged the Canadians."

Leroux cursed. If the Canadians were under attack, that five-minute estimate was meaningless.

En Route to Presidential Motorcade

Mexico City, Mexico

Dwyer fired several bursts at the intersection ahead from the passenger-side window of a commandeered SUV. They had acquired eight vehicles from airport security, but unfortunately, none of them were up-armored. If they took a direct hit in the wrong spot, they were screwed.

The front loader slammed into another car lying across the road, shoving it aside with ease, the small convoy falling in behind it, weaving their way through the now opened passage. They had made excellent time, the enemy focusing on the main motorcade rather than the opposite end of the route. It was clear they had never planned on their prey making it this far.

The prime minister's life and that of the American president were now in his team's hands. The motorcade had taken a chance, cutting diagonally across the planned route, but now they were stuck without any means of clearing blockades ahead of them. It had been a bold move, one he would have taken as well, but if his team were stopped, it could mean the end of everything.

The loader continued forward, picking up speed, and the SUVs repositioned to flank it on either side as gunfire poured on them. What he would give for some air support right now, but unfortunately, the Apaches were still en route, not due to arrive until this would be over.

F-35s had reached the area and were circling overhead, but were useless down here on the ground. All they could do was make sure nothing got in the air that belonged to the enemy. They needed the gunships or some miracle to guarantee their path forward, but he was a firm believer in not relying on others. Assume the worst, assume no help was coming, assume your extraction will be late, assume the intel was wrong and you're facing double the enemy you were promised, assume equipment malfunction, assume every mission had the potential to be a Charlie Foxtrot.

Then plan accordingly and get yourself out of the quagmire.

"RPG! Rooftop, two o'clock!"

Dwyer spotted the hostile on a rooftop at the intersection ahead, the shoulder-launched projectile already aimed. He tilted his weapon up and fired, missing, though it was enough for the man to duck for cover, allowing someone else to get a bead on him when he popped back up. An assault rifle opened up from their left, a hostile having hidden in a doorway, waiting for the loader to pass. He cursed as the rear left tire was shredded. The gunman was taken out moments later, but it was already too late. The damage had been done and the loader ground to a halt.

They weren't making it on time.

Presidential Motorcade

Mexico City, Mexico

Atlas pumped the jack, raising one of the concrete barriers far too slowly for his liking. Niner and the others had returned with a wealth of supplies and were now at work. Niner, lying on his side, shoved a demolition saw underneath the barrier. "I'm in!" he shouted before firing up the blade, the screech of the diamond tip cutting edge slicing away at the metal bolt, music to Atlas' ears.

Something came in over the comms but he couldn't hear it over the din. He instead switched his attention to the next barrier as Spock continued to pump the other end of the one Niner was working on. Each barrier had two bolts and there were three barriers. Six bolts to cut and they would be out of the noose they found themselves in.

Heavy gunfire from the far end of the motorcade had Atlas concerned for his brothers, but he had to focus on the job at hand. If they succeeded, everyone would be saved. He continued pumping, his muscles bulging, and he thanked God for his intense workouts. It was difficult going, but he wasn't tiring, at least not appreciably. Spock moved on to the opposite end of the barrier Atlas was now working as Jimmy slid under the first, an angle grinder powering up, joining Niner's larger saw. Mickey and Jagger continued to struggle jacking the third when Niner's saw fell silent and the little man rolled clear.

"That's one done. Five to go."

Atlas jerked his chin toward the third and outermost barrier since there was no way to access the middle one he was working on while the first was in the way. "Get to work on that one. As soon as Jimmy finishes cutting the second bolt, we'll drag it out of the way."

Niner kept his customary one-liners to himself, instead repositioning, recognizing their critical situation.

"Did you guys hear that?" asked Spock, tapping his ear.

Atlas shook his head as he continued to raise the barrier. "No, what?"

"The Canadian front loader has been taken out. They don't have a new ETA."

Atlas cursed then redoubled his efforts. "Time to save ourselves, I guess."

Over Arlington, Virginia

Brooklyn Tanner stared at the laptop screen as their helicopter thundered toward their target. Langley had just sent them plans for the warehouse and surrounding area that they were about to hit. They had no idea how many they were facing, what they were armed with, or whether the baby they were being sent in to retrieve was still there or even alive.

She was the leader of Echo Team, a group of CIA elite operatives seconded to Homeland Security so they could operate on American soil. They were rarely deployed, but in this case, a CIA hunch had her team closest to the ball, and there weren't many balls more important than the sitting president's kidnapped child.

"Two minutes!" shouted the pilot.

"Copy that!" she replied. "Equipment check!"

Her team inspected their weapons and gear as a crewmember slid open the door to their Black Hawk. They were inserting half a mile away to reduce the chances of tipping off the hostage takers. She would prefer farther since the Black Hawk was not known for being quiet, but at half a mile, they were already looking at several minutes to cover the distance. Inserting a mile or more out with all their gear could mean the difference between life and death for the baby.

She turned to the others. "Okay, ladies and gents, I hope you've been keeping up with your cardio. We're not jogging in, we're sprinting in. Seconds could count here. If anyone gets a stitch or sprains an ankle, we're leaving you behind. First six that get there begins the assault." She grinned. "But I intend to be the first."

Michael Lyons, her second in command, gave her a look. "I've seen you run. There's no way you're beating me."

"I've been practicing. Prepare to have your ass handed to you."

He laughed. "Challenge accepted."

The chopper pulled up, the nose tilting high as the pilot killed the forward momentum of the massive airframe. They dropped to the ground, hitting with a bounce, and Tanner jumped out then cleared the rotors, getting a bearing from her helmet's visor. She checked to see her entire team had successfully inserted, then pointed toward their target, breaking out into a sprint before the chopper had lifted off.

Please, God, let the kid be alive.

Vice President's Office, The White House

Washington, D.C.

Terri had thrown up when she saw the photo sent by the cartel. It was Thomas' baby lying on a table with a large pot of water sitting atop a campfire grill just beginning to boil. Thomas had managed to keep her cool, threatening all-out war against the cartels if anything happened to her child now that she had issued the pardons.

"Until I'm shaking my brother's hand, you haven't fulfilled your end of the bargain," had been the response.

Stottlemeyer entered the room, still oblivious to what was truly going on. Terri wiped her eyes dry and Thomas remained seated behind her desk, gripping a picture frame that held a photo of her family.

"I've got an update for you, Madam President."

Thomas pushed the frame aside. "What is it?"

"Fortunately, all the people you pardoned are still being held at the same prison. We haven't had time to transfer them yet to different facilities. I've made it clear to the warden that their expedited release is essential, otherwise the cartels won't break off the attack in Mexico City. He's agreed to let the paperwork follow, and all eleven are already being transferred and should be heading for the airport in less than ten minutes, where we've chartered a private jet to take them to Mexican airspace."

"How long will that take?"

"I'm told it's ten minutes to the airport, five minutes to get them in the air, ten minutes to Mexican airspace, since they're in Texas. Depending on where the cartels want them to land, this could all be over in less than an hour."

Thomas frowned, glancing over at the televisions playing the news. "I don't know if they've got an hour." She exhaled heavily. "Let every news organization in the country know what airport they're leaving from. I want their arrival and departure broadcast worldwide so that the cartels can see what's happening. Maybe that'll buy the president a reprieve."

"Yes, ma'am, I'll see to it."

Stottlemeyer left and Thomas regarded Terri. "Do you think he knows?"

"Knows what, ma'am?"

"About my baby."

Terri shrugged. "If he does, he's certainly not letting on. And the news report only broke a few minutes ago and he's been busy. Even if he does know, does it make a difference? He's still going to execute your orders now that the pardons have been issued, no matter what he thinks the motivations are."

Thomas slumped in her chair. "Let's hope you're right. We can't afford for anything to go wrong."

Presidential Motorcade

Mexico City, Mexico

"Everyone clear!" ordered Atlas as he stepped back.

Everyone working on the barriers moved away and Atlas signaled for the SUV chained to the first concrete block to proceed. The driver gave a thumbs-up and the engine revved. The truck pulled back, the chain tautening, the engine straining against the heavy load before it finally slid along the pavement. Cheers erupted as the first blockage pulled out of the way, and the moment it was clear, Atlas leaped back into action.

"Let's go! Let's go! We've still got two more!"

Niner dropped into position, as did Jimmy, both of them firing up their saws to cut away the bolts holding the center barrier that they hadn't been able to access until now.

Atlas activated his comms. "Zero-One, Zero-Seven. The first barrier is clear. Working on the second, over."

"Copy that, Zero-Seven," replied Dawson, the gunfire heavy on the other end. "How long till you have the other two cleared?"

"Assuming you can keep the fighting at your end, I estimate no more than five minutes. Hopefully we can get that down to three."

"Copy that, Zero-Seven. Let's go for that three number, shall we? We're already being forced to fall back."

"Copy that. You'll have your three minutes if I have to pick the things up myself."

"Copy that, Zero-Seven. I'm sorry I'll miss the gun show. Zero-One, out."

Atlas steadied the barrier Niner was working under just in case the jack failed. There was no way in hell he could save his friend from being crushed, but there was no way he wouldn't tear every muscle trying.

Speeding things up meant making things more dangerous.

Arlington, Virginia

Tanner cursed as Lyons beat her to the warehouse, though only by a few paces.

"Beers are on you," huffed Lyons as the rest of the team caught up, everyone sucking air.

She activated her comms. "Control, Echo Zero-One. We're at the warehouse. Any change in status, over?"

"Negative, Zero-One. Nobody has come or gone since you inserted, over."

"Copy that." She indicated for her team to position for the breach and they broke off as she and three of her team took up position by a side door, one of them prepping a battering ram. The other two teams reported they were in position and she steeled herself for what was to come. "Control, Zero-One, we're ready to breach, over."

"Copy that, Zero-One. Killing the power and comms now." There was a pause. "You're clear to breach, over."

"Acknowledged, Control. Echo Team, breach! Breach! Breach!"

The battering ram swung and the door splintered open. Tanner rushed in, clearing right, followed by the others. She flipped down her night vision goggles, the warehouse dark save for a couple of emergency lights and narrow slivers of sunshine from the three breached entrances. A hot heat source was just to her left as she surged forward, her MP5 raised, and her mouth filled with bile at the realization it was a boiling pot of water.

She opened fire, taking out any heat source the size of an adult. The last hostile dropped as she advanced toward the table with the boiling pot of water, the heat radiating off it hiding any other heat source that might be nearby. There was a bundle sitting beside the burner, but she didn't see a baby anywhere.

"Secure the area. Make sure there's no one else in here. Control, Zero-One, turn the lights back on, over." The lights flickered on a moment later and she flipped up her goggles, taking in the scene. Half a dozen hostiles were dead or dying. "Does anyone see the kid?"

A string of negatives replied as she reached the roiling pot of water. She closed her eyes for a moment, saying a silent prayer, then leaned in, peering into the pot. It was empty.

The bundle beside the pot sitting on the table moved. She reached over and gently pulled aside what turned out to be a pile of laundry, and cried out in relief at the sight of the baby, squirming for attention. She picked her up and held her, tears in her eyes. She sucked in a breath through her nose, steadying herself. "Control, Zero-One, let the president know we have her baby and she's unharmed, over."

"Copy that, Zero-One. Good job. It's nice to finally have something go well for a change."

"Amen to that."

En Route to Presidential Motorcade

Mexico City, Mexico

Dwyer emptied his mag into the engine block of the Toyota pickup, bringing it to a steaming halt as two other team members took out the gunner in the back, the .50 cal bolted to the bed falling silent. The loader continued to move forward, though at a much slower pace, what remained of the tread from the shot-out tire rapidly shredding. Soon it would be a metal rim carving long lines into the asphalt, but they were almost there, less than a mile to go, and behind them lay a cleared route all the way to the airport.

Half his men, including himself, were on foot now, the vehicles they had been in disabled. It meant they were exposed, and two of his men were already wounded. Unfortunately, not only were they rapidly losing vehicles, they were burning through their ammo. The longer this went on, the more likely it was they would need rescuing themselves.

The loader slammed into another car, shoving it aside, the grinding of the rear tire overwhelming the gunfire for a few moments. His man behind the controls leaned out, pointing ahead. "It's clear all the way to the American position!"

"Keep going. Apparently they've got a barrier that needs to be cleared." He received a thumbs-up and the crippled machine continued forward. "Control, Sierra Leader. We've got a clear shot to the American position. Let them know friendlies are coming in from the north, but we're actively engaged with hostile forces, over."

"Copy that, Sierra Leader, relaying your status now, over."

They continued forward, the going far slower than it had been, but they were almost there, and once they were, they would have the safety of the armored convoy vehicles plus air support that was only a few minutes out. This was almost over.

Then he was definitely taking a vacation.

Presidential Motorcade

Mexico City, Mexico

Atlas and Niner high-fived as the second barrier was pulled out of the way. Jimmy and Spock rushed in, connecting the chains to the third that had already been cut loose, a second SUV's engine roaring as they pulled the final barrier free.

Atlas activated his comms. "Zero-One, Zero-Seven. The barriers have been cleared, over."

"Copy that, Zero-Seven. Get the motorcade moving. You should be able to see the Canadians coming in from the north, over."

Atlas spotted a wheeled loader limping toward them, escorted by several SUVs and a dozen men on foot. "Copy that, Zero-One. I've spotted the Canadians, over."

"Acknowledged, Zero-Seven. Coordinate with them on our meetup. I'll be bringing up the rear, over."

"Copy that, Zero-One." Atlas turned to the group. "Let's go! Let's go! Let's go! We've got a clear shot to the airport thanks to the Canadians. Let's not let it go to waste."

The first SUV pulled through the gap in the barrier and Atlas jumped onto the running board. "Control, Zero-Seven, let the Canadians know that we're approaching from their south. We've cleared the barrier, over."

"Copy that, Zero-Seven, relaying the message now and integrating comms. You'll be able to coordinate directly, over."

"Copy that. Sierra Leader, do you read, over?"

The Canadian team lead replied immediately. "Affirmative. I read you."

"This is Bravo Zero-Seven, hanging onto the side of that lead SUV coming toward your position. What's your situation, over."

"I've got two wounded and four civilian vehicles barely roadworthy, but I also have a clear path all the way back to the airport, over."

"Copy that. Abandon any vehicles that you don't think can make it, then hitch a ride with any of ours."

"Be advised, Zero-Seven, we're under heavy attack and running low on ammo, over."

"Copy that. You can resupply when we reach you. Suggest you fall back toward the airport, that'll allow us to pass through the enemy position faster, then we'll pick you up once we catch up to you, over."

"Copy that, Zero-Seven. Sierra and Tango Teams falling back toward the airport. Good luck."

"Good luck to you. Zero-Seven, out."

Atlas peered ahead to see the Canadian vehicles turning around, those on foot sprinting in the opposite direction, the enemy gunfire quieting as they assumed they were victorious. Atlas spotted the enemy ahead, dozens stepping out into the open, their backs to the approaching motorcade, guns held high in the air as they cheered.

"Zero-Seven to Ground Team, hold your fire at the head of the column until we're engaged, then maintain fire until we're clear of the approaching enemy position. Pick up any Canadian stragglers on the way. They were kind enough to clear a path for us, I think the least we can do is give them a lift home, over."

Dawson's voice chirped in his ear. "This is Bravo Zero-One and I approve of this message, over."

Atlas laughed and readied his weapon as they rapidly closed in on their unsuspecting enemy.

One last challenge, then they were home free.

Garza Cartel Compound

Copper Canyon, Mexico

Garza downed a shot of tequila, celebrating with the rest in the room at the sight of his brother and the other cartel leaders climbing into the back of a bus, all free men, all innocent of any past crimes, thanks to him. But what thanks would he get? His brother would be back here perhaps in as little as an hour, then things would go back to normal. His brother would be running things and he would be a glorified errand boy, yet again begging for scraps.

It wasn't right. He should be running the family. His brother was barely a year older and could never have pulled off what he had just pulled off. He had been fielding calls all day from the other cartels congratulating him on what he had accomplished, and now that the big bosses were being released thanks to him, he expected another deluge of congratulatory messages to begin pouring in. Right now, he was the boss of bosses, but as soon as his brother landed, it would all be over, his brief taste of power ended, not because of failure but because of success.

It definitely wasn't right.

One of his men entered the room and walked over, concern on his face. He leaned in and whispered. "I can't reach our team in Virginia."

"The baby?"

"I don't know. Their orders were to kill it if they were hit, but there's no way to know."

"Get some eyes on the warehouse to see what's happening. We might have just lost our biggest bargaining chip."

Presidential Motorcade

Mexico City, Mexico

Niner clung to the side of the lead SUV, Atlas opposite him on the driver's side, his M4 ready as they accelerated toward their still-celebrating enemy. It was tempting to fire now, but the closer they got, the more guns that would come into play from his brothers behind them, and the better angle they would have on those tucked into the side streets. Eventually, someone would spot them—their good fortune couldn't last forever.

"Open fire!" came Atlas' voice over the comms.

Niner didn't bother looking over at his friend to see what had caused him to give the order. Instead, he simply fired on full auto, mowing down their unsuspecting enemy as more weapons behind them joined the fray. It was a slaughter. And after everything they had been through over the past hour, and what their country had been through this week, it was almost cathartic bringing justice to some of those responsible.

Bullets tore at the hood and Niner ducked, searching for the source. He spotted muzzle flashes from a window just ahead, three stories up, and radioed it in. "Shooter on the third floor of the blue building on the right. Heavy machine gun."

He adjusted his aim but didn't quite have the angle. Atlas swung his M4 toward the target then squeezed the trigger, several bursts of hot lead sent toward the elevated position. Small bursts of pulverized concrete peppered the stone around the window before Atlas found his mark, the gun falling silent, its owner collapsing over the windowsill. They continued forward, traveling at a good clip now, the Canadians just ahead.

"Sierra Team, Bravo Zero-Seven. We're coming up on your six now. I've got room for two on the lead vehicle, left and right, over."

"Copy that, Zero-Seven."

Atlas tapped on the windshield, looking down at the driver and pointing ahead. "Slow down. Two to pick up."

Niner spotted the thumbs-up response and braced himself as the vehicle rapidly slowed and two Canadians jumped on board. Niner glanced back to see one of them was MWO Dwyer.

"You good?" asked Atlas.

"Yeah. Just get me to the head of my team and I'll switch off."

"Copy that."

The enemy gunfire was now behind them, the Canadians having cleared the way directly ahead. All they had to do now was to pick up everybody, then hammer it all the way to the airport.

Piece of cake.

"RPG!" shouted one of the Canadians and Niner's eyes bugged out as the warhead streaked toward them.

Well, it was fun while it lasted.

He dove off the running board just as the driver jerked the wheel to the left, swerving to avoid the incoming RPG. He hit the ground with a grunt, rolling to absorb the impact, ducking as the projectile detonated against the side of a building, having narrowly missed its intended target.

Niner swung around, his M4 raised, taking in the scene ahead as a second RPG slammed into the engine compartment of what had been his ride out of here, bringing the vehicle to an abrupt halt. His immediate thoughts were of Atlas, but there was nothing he could do about that right now as at least a dozen hostiles charged from buildings on either side of the street, all carrying shoulder-launched weapons.

He opened up on the ones in his arc, a second gun joining the battle behind him, a Canadian C8, allowing him to narrow his area of responsibility. Two more RPGs streaked toward them and Niner dropped, firing wildly, hoping for a lucky shot, and he got one, one of the warheads exploding, though too close, the blast knocking him onto his back.

His world faded as a loud ringing in his ears overwhelmed him. Somebody grabbed him by the vest and hauled him up.

"You still with us?"

It was Atlas. He was sure of it. Though the voice was distant, there was no mistaking the impossibly deep timbre. A meaty hand smacked him on the cheek.

"Are you with me?"

Niner gulped, his eyes opening, his friend's concerned face staring at him.

"You good?"

"Give me a kiss."

Atlas tossed him back onto the pavement. "You're good."

Heavy gunfire and explosions greeted his reawakening. He pushed to a knee, crouching low as he did a self-assessment. His hearing was slightly impaired, but he didn't appear to be injured. The SUV he had been riding on smoldered to his left, all four doors opened. He couldn't see anybody inside, which hopefully meant everyone had survived. Four SUVs were spread out and the Delta teams were heavily engaged all around him.

"Watch your fire!" shouted Atlas. "We've got friendlies coming in from the north." He glanced back at Niner. "You in this fight?"

Niner gave a quick nod, his hearing rapidly improving. "I'm in."

"Then get in it!"

Niner advanced, taking a position on Atlas' left. He opened fire on a nearby doorway. "Where are they coming from?"

Atlas fired. "Control reports there's nobody on the opposite streets. It looks like they had set up this ambush before we even got underway. This is where they intended to stop us if we made it this far. A lot of heavy weapons are mounted inside the buildings. Plus, it seems like everyone and their dog has an RPG."

"Where's that air support?"

"Two minutes out. BD's given orders to have them target the other side of the buildings and bring them to the ground."

"That should do the trick. So, I guess that means we're not going in to clear them?"

"Not unless you want to be in there when it comes down on you."

"I think I'll pass." Niner continued to fire, as did Atlas, when Dawson rushed up beside them, taking a knee.

"Ladies, sit rep."

An explosion tore apart the side of the building just ahead and Atlas gestured toward it. "We managed to confiscate some grenades, so now that we've got some of our own in the mix, they're starting to keep their heads down. We've already got at least half a dozen casualties. Nothing serious so far, but our luck's not gonna hold out forever, and we can't risk bringing the president through this until these buildings are taken care of."

Dawson agreed with Atlas' assessment. "Keep them pinned inside the buildings and make sure everyone's got a ride. As soon as those Apaches arrive and distract these guys, we're out of here."

"Copy that. You say the word and we're history."

Dawson slapped Atlas on the back then returned to the rear where the remainder of their force was defending the president, prime minister, and everyone else from being overwhelmed by the bulk of the enemy force pressing from behind.

Niner continued his suppression fire on the windows and doorways surrounding them, mentally counting down those two minutes, while glancing over to his left to pick which chariot he would ride out of here.

Dawson sprinted back to the rear of the column where Red was holding down the fort with Charlie and Foxtrot teams. He stopped at the SUV with Special Agent Carlyle, who rolled down his window.

"How's it look up there?"

"Like a shit show, but the road's still clear. It's just too risky to bring the president through it. Everybody has an RPG up there, plus they've got fifty cals mounted on both sides of the road inside the buildings. It's a gauntlet, and we don't have Clint Eastwood's bus."

Carlyle laughed. "I know what movie I'm watching when I get home."

"The Gauntlet?"

"No, The Little Mermaid with my daughter. There's no way in hell I want to see a gun for at least a week."

Dawson laughed. "Sounds like a plan. Those Apaches should be hitting in less than sixty seconds. Make sure everyone's ready. Once they engage, we're going to have a very narrow window while they're distracted trying to save their own asses. Just make sure you guys are loaded up with my men. I don't want anyone left behind."

"I'll make you a deal, Sergeant Major. Something tells me you're the last man out in any of these situations. I'm your ride. We don't go until you go."

Dawson slapped the man on the shoulder. "Until the bitter end, then."

"Bravo Zero-One, Control. Apaches are about to engage, over."

Dawson tapped his ear. "Copy that, Control. Apaches engaging. Bravo Zero-One to Ground Team. Apaches are about to engage. This is it, people. Continue suppression fire, then as soon as Bravo Zero-Seven gives the command, everyone grab a vehicle and head for the airport. Just make sure no one gets left behind. Good luck to us all."

"Suppression fire!" shouted Atlas as he opened up on the windows around them, the bulk of Alpha and Bravo teams, along with what remained of two Canadian units, pouring lead and grenades on the enemy positions.

"Ground Team, this is Control. Apaches engaging, over."

Atlas smiled at Niner as rocket fire and chain guns pounded the area on the opposite side of the buildings they were trapped between. It took a few moments for their enemy to realize what was happening before the gunfire dwindled, the ground vibrating as the unrelenting assault punished the city.

"Continue suppression fire!" he ordered as he slowly rose, assessing the situation. This was it. He activated his comms. "This is Bravo Zero-Seven to Ground Team. Find a ride and maintain suppression fire until we're clear. We leave in ten seconds, over."

Atlas jumped on the side of the new lead SUV. Niner climbed on the other side, two Canadians joining them. His mental countdown reached zero and he slammed on the roof.

"Let's go! Let's go! Let's go!"

The driver hammered on the gas, launching them through thousands of shell casings and random debris, none of it big enough to impede their progress. Atlas continued to fire bursts at the buildings lining the road as they picked up speed. He glanced back to see a trail of vehicles behind them, four Ground Team members on each, as they put some distance between the ambush site and themselves. He smiled at the sight of the Apaches continuing their unrelenting assault.

Maybe they would make it out of this alive.

Dawson surveyed the area one last time as he and Red hopped onto the running board of Carlyle's SUV, the man having remained behind as promised. He smacked the roof. "Let's go!"

"You don't have to ask us twice," replied Carlyle, the driver pressing on the gas, sending them surging after the last of the motorcade. Dawson's eyes searched the area, watching for any stragglers, any wounded, any dead, determined to leave no one behind, as Red did the same on the opposite side. The Apaches continued punishing the enemy just ahead. They were about to enter the gauntlet laid down for them.

"This is Bravo Zero-One. Continue suppression fire until we're clear of the main combat area, over."

The gunfire that had dwindled picked back up. They might be firing at nothing, but all it would take was one lucky bastard to get off an RPG and the president could be dead and all this would have been for nothing. His M4 rattled as he sprayed the facade of the buildings they passed, the motorcade picking up speed. They had less than five miles to get to the airport and apparently a clean shot. If they could maintain thirty miles per hour, they could be there in five or six minutes, which to him sounded impossibly sweet, considering how slow a go they had had of it so far.

It had felt like an eternity, as if they had been fighting for hours if not days, yet the whole thing was barely an hour, though so much had happened in that hour. People had died, people had been wounded, people had been traumatized for life. A city smoldered and a country's leadership had changed. When he got out of this, he just hoped Washington would let America get its revenge.

He wanted Garza dead, and he wanted to be the one to deliver justice.

A .50 cal opened up on them and Dawson crouched on the running board.

"Two o'clock!" shouted Red.

Dawson spotted the target and opened fire, forcing the gunner to fall back inside as they raced past his position. He continued to fire, and moments later they were clear, the gauntlet behind them, the Apaches breaking off their attack, two racing over the motorcade to take up positions ahead while the other two covered them from behind.

Red grinned at him. "Is it too soon to celebrate?"

A shot rang out, a single shot out of the tens of thousands fired today, and Dawson gasped as Red fell off the opposite side of the vehicle, tumbling onto the pavement before coming to rest in a crumpled heap.

And Dawson cursed the god supposed to protect men like them.

Belme Residence, West Luzon Drive

Fort Liberty, North Carolina

Shirley screamed as her husband fell off the SUV. He rolled several times, the cameraman zooming in on the lifeless figure, an anonymous soldier to the world watching the live action, but to everyone in the room, it was Master Sergeant Mike Belme, Red to his friends and brothers, loving husband and doting father.

Maggie wrapped an arm around Shirley's shoulders then gasped as her own husband dove off and hit the ground rolling as the SUV hammered on its brakes. Dawson rose then sprinted toward his friend as the distance grew between the cameraman and the rear of the motorcade. It didn't surprise her at all that her husband would be the last one to leave the fight. He would have made sure that nobody was left behind, and it was equally unsurprising that his best friend would be at his side.

Shirley clasped her hands in front of her mouth, her tears flowing. "Please, God, let him be all right. Please, God, let him be all right."

For most of them, this was the first time any had seen the men in their lives in action, and this was exactly why it should never happen. No one should see the person they loved killed on live TV.

Vanessa pointed and leaped to her feet. "He's alive!"

The camera cut away, the cameraman too far to maintain the shot, and he repositioned, the broadcast now showing a view through the windshield of the cameraman's vehicle.

Shirley stared at Vanessa. "Are you sure?"

Vanessa's head bobbed furiously. "Yes. He sat up just as BD reached him. I'm sure of it."

Maggie grabbed the remote from Shirley's trembling hands and backed up the live broadcast. Everyone leaned in, the camera bobbing furiously due to the extreme zoom. Dawson slowed up as he reached Red's body. Everyone leaned in closer, breaths collectively held, when the downed warrior sat up abruptly. Everyone shot to their feet, screams of joy and relief released, and Maggie hugged Shirley hard as the woman hopped up and down in excitement.

Hugs, high fives, and fist bumps were exchanged when somebody noticed the phone was ringing. Shirley picked it up and checked the call display. "It's my doctor." The joy from a moment ago was stowed as she took the call. "Hello?"

Maggie strained to hear the other end of the conversation but couldn't.

"I understand, tomorrow at 9:00 AM. No, it'll just be me. My husband…" Shirley hesitated. "He's not available."

Maggie reached out and took Shirley's hand, mouthing, "I'll go with you."

A tear escaped, rolling down Shirley's cheek, catching on her chin before dropping onto her shirt. "A friend will come with me. Yes, doctor, I understand. Goodbye."

"What did he say?"

Shirley dropped the phone on the couch and leaned forward, her shoulders rolling inward, shaking as she sobbed, her hands clasped over her face. "It's—" She gasped, unable to finish her sentence. She sniffed hard, steeling herself to deliver the news that everyone in the room could already guess. "It's cancer."

Presidential Motorcade

Mexico City, Mexico

Dawson cried out in relief as he dropped to a knee beside his best friend, now sitting up. "I thought you were dead."

Red extended a hand. "We will be if we don't get the hell out of here."

Dawson hauled Red to his feet and gave him the once-over. "What happened?"

"Caught a round straight in the chest, knocked me off the damn running board. Took me a few moments to catch my breath. I think I might have cracked my noodle, too."

Dawson ran his fingers over his friend's bald scalp then twisted Red's head to the side, tapping a welt. "Does that hurt?"

"Ow! Yes!"

"Good, it means you're still alive. Now, let's get the hell out of here so a medic can take a proper look at that."

Their driver had backed up and Red resumed his position on the running board as Dawson climbed on the other side, slapping on the roof. "Let's go!"

The gunfire was picking up behind them now that there was nobody left to provide suppression fire, but one of the Apaches that had hung back sent several lengthy bursts down either side of the road, as the SUV got underway, this time accelerating a little slower, the driver showing concern for Red's condition.

Dawson had his M4 ready but held his fire so he wouldn't need to reload while hanging on the side of a vehicle barreling down a debris-strewn road. The Canadians had cleared a path, but it wasn't a direct line, their driver forced to swerve in and out, threading the needle left behind. They continued to pick up speed, Red urging the driver on, assuring him he was okay.

Red pointed ahead. "There they are!"

Dawson smiled at the sight of brake lights ahead and he took a moment to focus on exactly where they were. He had memorized the route, all the landmarks along the way, and thanked God when the brake lights disappeared around a corner of what should be the final turn leading to the airport. "Less than a mile!" he shouted as the driver slowed, taking the turn hard then accelerating out of it. They rapidly caught up to the rear of the motorcade, the airport now in sight, the front of a long trail of vehicles now on the airport grounds, security waving them through.

They were going to make it.

Operations Center 2, CIA Headquarters

Langley, Virginia

"Holy shit!"

Leroux glanced over his shoulder at Child. "What?"

"I'm monitoring that tap that Sherrie installed. You gotta hear this." He tapped his keyboard then looked up at the overhead speakers as he replayed a conversation in Spanish.

"Don't worry, they're completely loyal to me. The president will never get on that plane."

"I've heard assurances like that before."

Leroux recognized the voice as that of Juan Garza. He mouthed the word "Juan" and Child gave a thumbs-up.

"Trust me, the Americans won't know what hit them. They don't stand a chance."

"You better be right about this. I'm not a big fan of failure."

"Neither am I."

The call ended and Leroux fit his headset in place. "Do we know who the second person is?"

"I'm running the voice now. Nothing yet."

"We need to find out." He stared at the feed, the motorcade now on airport grounds, the first vehicles coming to a halt near Air Force One, its occupants spilling out. A security cordon of Mexican police were lined up, their backs facing the action, no doubt watching for any hostiles that might be approaching.

Leroux reactivated his comms. "This is Langley Ops Center Two Control Actual to Delta Control Actual."

Clancy's voice replied. "This is Control Actual. Go ahead."

"We've intercepted a call between Juan Garza and an unknown male. We believe there might be a threat on the ground at the airport. The unknown male is assuring Garza that he has men that are completely loyal to him and that the president won't get on the plane alive."

"Stand by, Langley."

There was a click, and as more of the motorcade arrived, Clancy's voice cut in over a live channel. "This is Control Actual. We have credible intel that there may still be a threat to the president at the airport, over."

Dawson's voice replied. "Copy that, Control. Anything specific, over."

"Only that the reference was to men, not a man. I don't think we're dealing with a sniper here."

"Copy that, Control. This is Bravo Zero-One to Ground Team. Keep the president in his vehicle. I repeat, keep the president in his vehicle until we can lock down this scene."

"Bingo!" cried Child. "I've got him!"

A file photo appeared on the display along with the man's tombstone data. "He's Director General Fernando Trujilo, Internal Security."

"Holy shit!" exclaimed Packman. "It doesn't get more inside than that."

Leroux had to agree. Trujilo had control over everything involving the security operation. He would be why the cartels had known which route would be taken, what the other routes were so they could be blocked off just in case, and that the helicopters were just decoys.

He activated his comms. "Control Actual, we've identified the caller as Director General Fernando Trujilo, head of Internal Security."

Clancy cursed over the open comms, not bothering to acknowledge the report. Seconds could count. Trujilo had the power to control the entire security team at the airport.

There might not be a single person there they could trust.

Aeropuerto Internacional Benito Juarez

Mexico City, Mexico

Dawson rolled up to the parked motorcade, assessing the situation, the latest update from Clancy indicating they could be about to encounter a shitstorm. Something was off. Air Force One was to their left. A string of Mexican security spread from the nose and outward at a 45-degree angle, tilted toward the motorcade, another string from the tail enclosing the opposite end. If they were doing their job properly, there should be a third line protecting the motorcade at the base of what was essentially a triangle. But instead, there wasn't anybody there.

He cursed. There wasn't anybody there because they would be caught by their own friendly fire.

"This is Bravo Zero-One to Ground Team. The two Mexican security details are positioned to take us out without being caught in their own crossfire. On my mark, I want all drivers to open their doors except for the VIP vehicles. First sign of a hostile act, everyone opens fire. Take out both security details, then when clear, load the airplane. Pilot, if you're monitoring, the moment we begin to fire, be prepared to roll. Don't wait for any clearances from ATC, over."

"Copy that, Bravo Zero-One. We'll be ready."

Dawson positioned himself with Red on the opposite side of their SUV, facing the security detail on the left. All still had their backs to them, playing their part well. There was no point in tipping their hand until the president was vulnerable.

"This is Bravo Zero-One. Drivers, open your doors."

Dozens of doors opened all at once and one of the security detail flinched then spun around, raising his weapon. Another turned, triggered by his buddy.

"Open fire!" shouted Dawson as he squeezed the trigger. Scores of weapons, Canadian and American Special Forces along with American Secret Service joined in, belching hundreds upon hundreds of rounds at the would-be assassins. It was over in seconds, and Dawson rushed toward the president's SUV.

"This is Bravo Zero-One. Load the plane! I repeat, load the plane!"

Doors shoved open everywhere, civilians and VIPs sprinting toward the stairs. Dawson jogged alongside the president, his Secret Service detail providing a human shield as they helped the aging man to the stairs. Two agents grabbed him under the shoulders and carried him up the steps and inside as the massive 747's engines roared.

Dawson watched for the last of the delegation to hit the stairs then pointed at Dwyer. "Sierra and Tango teams next!"

Dwyer joined him at the bottom of the steps as his men sprinted up them and into the airplane, carrying the dead and wounded.

"Alpha team!" shouted Dawson as the last Canadian boot left the ground. He kept a wary eye on the area, but so far, it appeared Director General Trujilo had put all of his eggs in a single basket and lost. "Charlie Team then Foxtrot Team!" The security perimeter rapidly collapsed until it was finally only his men. "Bravo Team!" Dawson smacked each of his men on the back as he counted them off in his head.

Red unlocked the steps and the two of them pushed the ramp clear as the plane rolled. Niner and Atlas stood in the doorway, tossing ropes out. Red grabbed on, dragging himself up as Dawson did the same, the airplane continuing to taxi toward the runway. Red disappeared inside and moments later, hands grabbed Dawson and hauled him in. He tumbled out of the way as Atlas and Niner pulled up the ropes, then one of the flight crew sealed the door.

Dawson headed for the cockpit. "Any sign of trouble?" he asked, the cockpit door open.

"Not yet. The Mexicans are screaming in my ear that I'm not cleared, but they can go eff themselves." The pilot leaned forward and pointed up. "We've got company."

Dawson stepped forward and twisted his head. "F-35s, they're ours. They'll provide escort all the way home."

"Get out of my hair, Sergeant Major or whatever the hell rank you are. I've got a plane to fly."

Dawson smacked the man on the back and smiled. "Consider me gone." He left the cockpit as the plane made its final turn onto the runway, the pilot revving up to full power without stopping. They rapidly gained speed as Dawson joined Red and Special Agent Carlyle.

"Counts?"

"We've got everybody, including our dead."

Dawson frowned. "How many did we lose?"

Carlyle sighed. "I've got two dead and three wounded that should make it."

"Honcho from Alpha Team took an unlucky hit just above his vest. He's in the back," said a somber Red.

Dawson closed his eyes for a moment. He had fought, trained, and partied with the man for years. "He was a good friend. He'll be missed."

"Charlie and Foxtrot teams reported no dead but several wounded each."

"How did you guys make out?" asked Carlyle.

"We had a few close calls and there's gonna be some tender ribs." Dawson jerked a thumb at Red. "And this one has to have his noodle checked out, but we got lucky. Civilians?"

"Just one casualty."

"What was his name?"

"Her name. Florencia Torres. Her SUV was hit by an RPG. She survived the initial hit but she had a piece of shrapnel buried in her back that she didn't know about. She ended up bleeding out before they could save her."

The plane lifted off, chaff blasting from defense pods, and Dawson reached out and grabbed a handhold, as did the others. The pilot warned of a rapid ascent, cries and screams from the still panicked civilians reaching Dawson's ears, the terror heartbreaking, but they were alive when so many were dead. So many on both sides. And for what? What had been accomplished in the end? Nothing.

And unfortunately, he feared this war was far from over, and countless more were yet to die.

Garza Cartel Compound

Copper Canyon, Mexico

Garza shot out of his chair, screaming in rage at the video feed showing Air Force One leaving the ground, American fighter jets settling in on its wings providing escort. He grabbed the golden eagle statue off the bookshelf and hurled it at the screen, the panel shattering then falling off its mount and clattering onto the floor.

He had failed.

The door opened and Maria entered. "I take it you saw?"

He glared at her, his nostrils flaring. "Of course, I saw."

"And what are you going to do about it?"

"What do you mean?"

"Are you going to stand there like a little bitch and pout about things not working out, or are you going to take control of the message like we said?"

He inhaled hard, his glare easing somewhat. "And what's the message?"

"That you control the police, you control the military, you control Mexico City. You can shut it down whenever you want, that you are El Jefe de Jefes, the Boss of Bosses. You run this country and you run the streets of America."

Her words filled him with bravado. She was right. Every word of it. He did run this country. He did run the streets of America. He was the most powerful leader among the cartels, the boss of bosses. He frowned. Until his brother landed.

"What's wrong?"

"Everything you said is true for"—he checked his watch—"less than an hour. Once my brother, your husband, is on the ground, he is El Jefe and I'll just go back to being one of his minions."

Maria rounded the desk and placed her hands on his chest, staring up into his eyes. "Do you know why I married your brother?"

"His money?"

She shook her head. "His power, his strength, the fact that every man in any room he walked into trembled with fear." She reached up, clasping her fingers behind his neck. "I see in you what I once saw in him. *You* are El Jefe de Jefes. He never was." She pulled him closer. "You terrify me, and I find that extremely erotic."

He leaned in and kissed her, holding her tight, his hands caressing her forbidden body, the absolute power he held overwhelming, intoxicating, irresistible. And something he couldn't give up. He pushed her away and held up a finger before she could protest. He picked up his phone, dialing a number.

"Yes, boss?"

"Take it out."

"You got it, boss."

He ended the call.

"Who was that?" she asked as she dropped to her knees and unbuckled his belt.

"The man who's going to kill your husband."

A wicked smile spread as she reached her prize. "I guess then I'm all yours."

Operations Center 2, CIA Headquarters

Langley, Virginia

Cheers erupted throughout the room as Tong reported Air Force One had crossed into American airspace. The inner door to the operations center hissed open and their boss, Morrison, entered, the room falling silent as the man joined Leroux.

"I take it the president is back in US airspace?"

"Yes, sir." Leroux indicated the screen. "Just a few seconds ago."

"Good. You might be interested to know, because it'll have been released the moment he entered our airspace, that the president was sworn back in as our commander in chief. As soon as it was official, Vice President Thomas announced her resignation and issued a statement that she had been coerced by the cartels with the kidnapping of her baby, a baby that, thanks to you and your team, is now safe and sound back with her mother."

"And the pardons?"

"Presidential pardons are only reversible if the president is impeached. Now, Congress can impeach the vice president for what she did while president, however, you know how long those things take and you can't hold innocent men in jail while waiting weeks or months for politics to play out."

Tong turned. "Do you think they will impeach her?"

"Not for a moment. My guess is the president will pardon her and silently thank her for solving his problem. You never heard it from me, but he screwed up. He went big when he should have gone small, and the country paid the price."

Leroux pointed at the display, a shaky feed from a news crew at Los Mochis airport in Mexico, broadcasting a live shot of the jet carrying the eleven drug lords about to land as free men. "And what are we gonna do about them?"

"Nobody's saying yet, but—"

Tong gasped and shot out of her seat. Leroux's eyes bulged as a missile streaked from left to right on the screen before slamming into the aircraft as it made its final approach. A fireball of orange and black death chewed at the sky, debris raining down on the ground below, the question as to what would happen to the eleven men answered for them.

Leroux turned to Morrison. "Did we do that?"

Morrison shook his head. "Not that I'm aware of, but I suppose anything's possible." He headed for the door. "I have a feeling it's gonna be a late night."

Garza Cartel Compound

Copper Canyon, Mexico

Garza roared in ecstasy as he exercised his dominion over his late brother's wife, the purest demonstration of his ultimate power, a fantasy fulfilled in so many ways, and as he did things to her, unspeakable things he could never do with his wife, he reveled in the power, the power long overdue him. He was El Jefe de Jefes, and he was going to enjoy every moment of it for however long it lasted.

The room shook, everything rattling, and he stopped in mid-thrust. "What was that?"

Maria reached up and grabbed him. "I don't give a shit what it was! Don't stop!"

Another rumble, then another, each one getting louder, each one shaking the room more violently. He stepped back and pulled up his pants as someone hammered on the door. He grabbed Maria and shoved her under the desk as he zipped up his fly and rapidly buttoned his shirt.

"What is it?"

The door flung open and one of his men rushed in. "I think we're being bombed!"

"What?"

"I think we're being bombed!"

The hallway behind the man collapsed, dust billowing toward them, and the floor split at his feet. Maria screamed and the minion's eyes bulged as she scrambled from her hiding place, her naked body revealed.

"They can't touch us in here!" declared Garza as the room continued to shake violently. "They can't touch us in here!" he screamed as the ceiling above caved in, ending his short reign of terror as millions of tons of mountain came crushing down upon him.

Sherrie exchanged a high five with Rivas as dozens of bunker-busting cruise missiles slammed into the side of the mountain, burrowing through the rockface before detonating, shattering the rock deep inside. If anybody did manage to survive, they would suffocate to death in short order. The last missile delivered its payload and she peered through her binoculars, watching the dust settle, confirming what she already knew.

The entrance was gone, the mountainside pulverized.

She activated her comms. "Control, Skylark. Confirming successful delivery of the warheads. Initial assessment is that no one could have survived. You might wanna let the Mexicans know where they can find the bodies if they care to do a lot of digging, over."

Leroux responded. "Copy that, Skylark. Once you're secure, we have one final mission for you before bringing you home."

"What's that, Control?"

"Details on your target have been sent to your secure messenger. Washington has given orders that Director General Trujilo is to be eliminated. How long do you think it'll take you to get to Mexico City?"

She rose to her knees, checking her watch. "I think we can be in position by tomorrow, over."

"Copy that, Skylark, report back when you're underway with an exact ETA. Control, out."

She rose, as did Rivas. "Looks like we're going to Mexico City."

Rivas' eyebrows rose. "Oh, why?"

"Somebody needs to die."

"Goody. I hope it's not a cousin."

Cape Fear Valley Cancer Center

Fayetteville, North Carolina

Red rushed into the recovery room and cried out at the sight of his wife lying in bed, hooked up to monitors. Maggie sat in a chair in the corner with her e-reader and looked up with a smile, a smile that broadened as she spotted Dawson behind Shirley's husband. She leaped to her feet and gave Dawson a hug then a kiss as Red took his wife's hand in his, clasping it to his chest.

"Is she all right?" he asked, and Maggie turned to him, about to answer, when Shirley did it for her.

"I'm fine."

Maggie and Dawson joined them at the foot of the bed. "She is. I talked to the doctor and she said they got it all. It hadn't metastasized, so she'll be fine."

"Oh, thank God!" gasped Red. He kissed Shirley's hand. "I'm so sorry I wasn't there for you."

She tapped her heart. "You were here the whole time."

He ran his fingers through her hair. "Not the same thing."

"It was enough. Besides, you were most definitely out of the country."

"Oh? And what makes you say that?"

Shirley gave him a look. "Nice try, big guy, but I watched you get shot on live TV."

Red rubbed his chest and chuckled. "I knew that damn reporter was gonna be trouble."

"Did she make it?" asked Maggie. "Last we heard, she had been injured."

Dawson nodded. "Yeah, she's fine. I think she's already out of the hospital."

Shirley propped herself up in the bed, Red adjusting her pillow. "So, what happens now? Are we still at war?"

Dawson shrugged. "All I know is Bravo Team has a week off to let all the bumps and scrapes heal, and the Mexican cartels are in disarray right now. Without any real leaders, there'll probably be a lot of infighting, a lot of bad guys will die, and a lot of innocents along with them. Once they've sorted out their mess, the president will have a decision to make. But for now, things will probably go back to normal. If we are still going to treat them as terrorists, I have a funny feeling we're gonna take them on one cell at a time rather than everyone at once. We overachieved and too many paid the price for it."

Maggie hugged him. "Well, I'm just glad you're home. I'm not letting you out of bed for a week."

He grinned. "Sounds good to me, but you'll have to do one thing for me."

"Anything."

"Niner and Atlas have both asked for two trays of lasagnas for themselves. They're flexible on whether they pick them up tonight or tomorrow."

Maggie rolled her eyes and groaned. "Fine, when we get home, I'll make the lasagna, then you and I have a week-long date. I deserve to be compensated for having to watch what you do for a living on live TV."

Dawson grinned at Red and Shirley. "If you'll excuse us, I have to go home and compensate the hell out of my wife."

Maggie squealed. "Good times!"

THE END

ACKNOWLEDGMENTS

This one was a blast to write. I've had novice authors ask me how I write my action scenes, and my answer is simple. I picture it as a movie, then write what I see. I think this one would make a great movie, but I think it would need a big budget.

While writing this, I crossed an exciting milestone as a writer—I sold my 2,000,000th book. Thanks to everyone who contributed to that number over the past decade or so. It's been quite the ride.

As usual, there are people to thank. My dad for all the research, Ian Kennedy for some breaching and spec ops info, Brent Richards for some weapons info, Sterling Spor and the followers of the Facebook Fan Page for some construction equipment info, and, as always, my wife and daughter, my late mother who will always be an angel on my shoulder as I write, as well as my friends for their continued support, and my fantastic proofreading team!

To those who have not already done so, please visit my website at www.jrobertkennedy.com, then sign up for the Insider's Club to be notified of new book releases. Your email address will never be shared or sold.

Thank you once again for reading.

Made in the USA
Las Vegas, NV
04 September 2023

77046404R00198